Broken Land
A Brooklyn Tale

John Biscello

Reprint Published by Unsolicited Press
Copyright © 2018 by John Biscello

Cover Artwork: Cris Qualiana
Editor: Sophia Noulas

ISBN: 978-1-947021-46-4

This book is a work of fiction. The characters, places, incidents, and dialogue are the product of the author's imagination and are not to be construed as real, or if real, are used fictitiously. Any resemblance to actual events, locales, or persons, either living or dead, is purely coincidental.

Broken Land
A Brooklyn Tale

"Begin at the beginning...
and go on till you come to the end: then stop."
—Lewis Carroll, Alice in Wonderland

"All philosophy is homesickness."
–Novalis

PART I

THE PHANTOM ITCH

I

There's not really a name for what I do. I am not an investigative journalist, I am not a private eye. I am not a minstrel essayist. There are many things that I am not.

If I were forced to impose a designation upon what I do, I'd say I'm a ... curious. That's all. Just curious.

Anyway, if I had an office and it had been a rainy Tuesday, then a tragic blonde with legs like scissors strong enough to cut a flesh-and-blood man in half might have walked in ... but that's not the way this story begins.

This story begins with a phone call from Jimmy Barrone, a writer and old friend of mine, who I hadn't heard from in years. His voice was tight and choked with tears, as he gurgled—Still curious, Salvo?

I knew it was Jimmy, because he was the only one from the old neighborhood who still called me Salvo.

Jimmy, I said, long time no hear.

Jimmy's dead, Salvo. Do you understand? I'm dead.

I countered Jimmy's hysterics with good old-fashioned logic.

You're not dead, Jimmy, I said. You're talking to me on the phone, therefore you're alive. Got it?

Jimmy snuffled some kind of primitive response, and went on—I don't know who's who anymore, or what's what. I'm breaking apart, Salvo. Fractals. Twelve Jimmy's, then thirty-six, then forty-eight.

I followed the beat of Jimmy's math, and tried to get through to a singular Jimmy, the one I had known since childhood.

Jimmy, I said, before you go to pieces with all this radical subdivision, tell me exactly what you think is happening.

I'm not me, were the last words Jimmy spoke before the line went dead.

I called back: a busy signal.

I calmly hung up the phone and sat at my desk. I picked up my plastic pencil sharpener and began sharpening pencils (#2's, orange-yellow). It was what I did when I wanted to think things over, calmly.

While my curiosity had been piqued, and I fully intended to head over to Jimmy's place and see what I could find out, I was not going to rush into the matter. I was not one to rush into anything, even when a distress signal has been fired like a flare in my direction. I didn't trust distress-signals, especially when they came from writers. Especially writers who had been raised Catholic and had grown up in Brooklyn.

I also understood that anxiety and panic were highly contagious maladies. It was my responsibility to keep myself clean and healthy and sound. Which required exacting detachment. Too little and you were caught in a trap. Too much and you drifted away.

My cat, Keaton, an ash-gray beauty with lantern-yellow eyes, leaped onto my lap. He stared up at me, as if he wanted something.

What, I said.

He responded by switching his lean tail, side to side, like a pendulum.

My nails dug into Keaton's scalp and gave it a good scratch. Keaton purred, like a pigeon making love to a toy motorboat, and closed his eyes.

I sharpened pencil after pencil, while playing Jimmy's words over and over again in my head. I tried out various configurations. I rearranged the original sequence, broke them down into independent syllables, played the sentences backwards, as if trying to uncover a satanic message.

After my fourteenth pencil, and with none of the configurations amounting to a breakthrough, I rose to my feet. Keaton fell to the floor, gracefully. He gave me a cutting look, then padded away. I went into the bathroom, flossed, brushed my teeth, and gargled mouthwash. Then I flossed again.

I put on my shoes and hat and overcoat. I grabbed my pencil sharpener, and six unsharpened pencils, and stored them in my coat-pocket. Then I left for Jimmy's.

Outside, the night had teeth and it was raining. It suddenly dawned on me: it was Tuesday.

Maybe if I had an office, I reasoned to myself, a scissor-legged blonde would walk into it. You never know about these things.

II

Even though I hadn't seen Jimmy in several years, I was banking on the fact that he still lived in Coney Island. Jimmy loved Coney Island. Coney Island was Jimmy's sweetheart, his soulmate. He loved her for her gilded past, when she was queen of the prom. He loved her as she grew fatter and older and lost some of her looks. He loved her in her darkest and most depressed phases, when breakdowns started occurring on a regular basis.

I took the D train to Stillwell Avenue. The walk from the station to Jimmy's apartment was five blocks. The rain had picked up considerably. I walked along, under the El, its tracks weeping. Jimmy lived in a high-rise, one of those buildings with hundreds of windows, thousands of bricks and millions of secrets.

I walked through the square courtyard where a bunch of teenage boys were hanging out, playing music on a boombox set squarely on a bench, with an umbrella set up to shield it from the rain. A couple of the boys were wearing hoods, the others weren't. None of them seemed to be bothered by the rain. As long as the box was playing they'd be alright.

Evening, fellas, I said, and tipped my hat.

They looked at me as if I were a foot fungus.

I rang the bell: 3-C. The name Barrone was scratched out, only a fragment of a B faintly visible. No answer. I rang again and held down the button for an obnoxiously long time.

A voice, garbled in static, came over the intercom.

Who you looking for, it crackled.

I'm looking for Jimmy. Jimmy Barrone. Do I have the right apartment?

No response.

I'm looking for, I started, but was cut off by what sounded like a robot being electrocuted. There was a click and I pushed the glass door open. I stood in the doorway for a moment, letting the thick, bassy sounds rising thud-like from the boombox envelop me like an electric blanket. I wanted to thank the boys for providing such an excellent soundtrack, then remembered that I was foot fungus and continued on my way.

I climbed the stairs to the third floor, where Jimmy's apartment was. When I got to his door, I knocked, not expecting an answer, and not getting one. I turned the knob, expecting the door to be open, and it was. Two for two. A good start.

Jimmy, I called out.

Silence.

Jimmy's apartment smelled thickly of cigarette smoke and something else—something missing. My nose couldn't put a finger on what that smell, or un-smell was.

The apartment was in total darkness. Recalling the layout of Jimmy's place, I crossed from the foyer into the living room. I fumbled for and found a light switch on a lamp and clicked it on. The lamp was no ordinary lamp. It was Betty Boop. Her arms were elevated at 45° angles, holding the lampshade over her rotund head, which was now cast in silky bronze light. The light also set off the red dress she was wearing, giving it a luminous, old-Hollywood look. Betty's saucer-shaped eyes seemed to be looking directly into me. Maybe they were trying to tell me something.

I'll question you later, Miss Boop, I said, knowing that I wouldn't.

I surveyed the living room. No tell-tale signs of disturbance or disorder. I saw a phone on its cradle, set at angle on an end table. I picked it up. There was a dialtone.

While checking the other rooms, I found a second phone in the kitchen, and it too was working. Above the kitchen counter, near the fridge, I spotted a laminated photo of Gabriella, Jimmy's mother, taped to a panel. The photo had been given out as a memento at Gabriella's funeral. I stared at the photo and never before realized how much Gabriella resembled a catcher's mitt. Mostly in the cheeks and mouth.

To the left of the photo, rosary beads hung on a nail. I removed the beads and stuffed them in my pocket. I'm not overly superstitious, but you never know when rosary beads might come in handy.

I sat on Jimmy's recliner in the living room and waited. Instinct told me that Jimmy wouldn't suddenly turn up, but it felt good to be in an apartment that wasn't my own. I went to the fridge to fix something to eat. Not much there. In the freezer I found Pepperoni-and-Cheese Hot Pockets. I microwaved one on high for two minutes, then poured myself a glass of grape soda and went back to the recliner.

While eating, I looked at Betty Boop looking at me. The space between us lengthened, as did time. I went through Jimmy's records, which were stocked in crates on the living room floor. I wanted to hear something that would kick me in the ass and send me to the zoo. I settled on Led Zeppelin III. I tried playing the record at a modest volume, but that wasn't doing the trick so I turned it up full-blast. Now there were fuzzy reverberations. Now there were tingles.

I nuked another Hot Pocket and poured myself another glass of grape soda. This time I added ice. I was in no rush to leave. Music sounded better in other people's homes. Food tasted better. Drinks drank better.

It was in the middle of "Immigrant Song" when a woman appeared in the doorway of the living room.

III

What are you doing here, she shouted over the music.

I could ask you the same question, I shouted back.

So I did.

What are you doing here?

We looked at each other, unsure as to who should answer first. Playing the gentleman, I decided it should be me.

I went to the stereo and turned off the music. Then I said—I'm a friend of Jimmy's. I came to check on him.

The woman, who remained a statue in the doorway, regarded me suspiciously.

I wiped my Hot-Pocket-stained fingers on my pants, then stepped forward slowly, so as not to alarm her, and extended my hand. I'm Salvatore Massimo Lunezzi. But you can call me Sal.

The woman looked at my hand, as if it were toxic, then looked into my eyes and saw me as no better than my hand. I let my hand fall limply to my side.

The woman remained still and silent and performed invasive surgery on me with her eyes. I didn't know where to turn, as it felt like she was stripping off my skin, bit by bit. After a long torturous minute of this, I was thoroughly ashamed of the fact that I existed.

I tried to crack wise—See anything you might find useful—but my voice betrayed me. It had come from a thirteen-year-old boy blindsided by puberty.

Suddenly, the woman's features softened and her icy demeanor melted.

I'm Anna, she said, in such a friendly voice it made me go

jelly inside. She smiled extra-big, then extended her tapered ivory fingers for me to shake. I clumsily groped her fingers and shook. Her hand was soft and clean-feeling.

For those of you who might be wondering: Anna was not a scissor-legged blonde. She had dark hair. Real dark. Like a night-forest with no moon. The color of her hair violently contrasted her skin, which was white. Real white. Like bleached bones. Or virgin snow. There was something very classical, very noble, about Anna's facial structure. Especially her nose, which reigned as the stately matriarch over the rest of her features.

Anna breezed by me and sat in the recliner. I couldn't take my eyes off her dress. It was an aquatic green with scalloped white trim. It puffed and flared and possessed the character of a decadent pastry. Ornate, pretentious, crème-filled.

Hungry, she said, and gave me a smiling look.

My face and hands grew hot and itchy. Had she seen into the depravity of my pastry association?

Then, with a quick sideways glance, she indicated the plate on which I had eaten the Hot Pocket, and said—What'd you have?

Hot Pocket, I said, relieved by what she didn't know.

Anna fished out a nail file from some secret pocket in her dress and began filing her glassy nails. This put me at ease and I sat down on the couch, facing her.

Mind if I sharpen a pencil?

Anna gestured—Be my guest.

I took out a pencil and my pencil sharpener and went to work. Shavings collected in the seashell ashtray set on the coffee table in front of me.

Keeping her eyes focused on her manicure, Anna said—I had to look you over in that way. Just to make sure.

I recalled her eyes and what they'd done and felt a

renewed wave of shame.

What were you making sure of, I asked.

That you really were Jimmy's friend.

Me and Jimmy grew up on the same block in Bensonhurst, I volunteered. Where you from?

Not Bensonhurst, Anna said, still not looking at me.

I kept at her. You Jimmy's ladyfriend?

Anna laughed like I had hit her with a funny stick.

By ladyfriend, what do you mean, she said.

I don't know, I said.

I'm not Jimmy's I-don't-know. Nor am I his main squeeze, as the phrasing goes. Like you, I'm Jimmy's friend.

Anna blew nail-dust off the tips of her fingers. I stared at those fingers as they extended fully. They were like unfinished sentences implying something poetic.

Sal, Anna started and paused.

That pause, which I believe was intentional, allowed me to reflect on how it was the first time Anna had spoken my name aloud. The effect was dizzying. Like she had given birth to me, signed the birth certificate and baptized me all in one syllable.

Anna continued. Do you know what's going on in Jimmy's life?

No, I confessed, point-blank. I set down my sharpened pencil and went to work on a second one.

Why do you think he called you, Anna said.

I guess because—I started, then stopped cold in my tracks.

I hadn't told Anna that Jimmy had called me. I felt the rotation of my pencil-sharpening intensify.

I'd like to know more about—I began, but Anna set her eyes on me, a couple of onyx watchdogs, and her sharp voice quickly cut me off—It's important that you answer my questions, Salvo, and not question them.

Salvo, I repeated to myself. I was now completely freaked out. I quickly scribbled a reminder on the blackboard in my mind—Anxiety and Panic are highly contagious maladies. Exacting detachment will serve you well.

In a composed manner I rose, and in a steady voice I said—Excuse me Anna, but I need to use the bathroom.

Of course, Anna said, in a too-sweet voice, and went back to her manicure.

When I got to the bathroom I took out the miniature travel toothbrush that I always carried in my inside coat pocket, and a travel-sized tube of toothpaste, and brushed my teeth vigorously. I opened Jimmy's medicine cabinet to see if he had any mouthwash. Bingo. Listerine. It was Cool Mint, the blue kind, and not Citrus, the orange kind. I didn't like Cool Mint but at least it wasn't Original, the pale gold kind, which I detested.

I gargled and spit into the sink. I lifted the toilet seat and sat down. I clutched the rosary beads in my hand and went over what Anna had said to me. After a couple of minutes I simplified things in my head and managed to re-assert my grip on what had gone down so far.

Jimmy had called me, out of the blue, worried that he was breaking apart. Twelve then thirty-six then forty-eight. His last words were, I'm not me, then the line went dead. I took a train to Jimmy's apartment, got buzzed into the building by an anonymous tenant, and entered Jimmy's unlocked apartment. I was listening to "Immigrant Song" when Anna appeared. Anna, the exquisite pastry, with mysterious ways. Anna, who was, I imagined, still sitting in the recliner, paring down her nails.

The turnings of my mind made me feel sleepy and alert at the same time. Or maybe it was the Hot Pockets and grape soda. I leaned back against the toilet tank. I let my gaze wander lazily from object to object. The towel rack, the red towel hanging from the rack, the tiles, the balled-up pile of clothes near the hamper, the hamper, the black thing set on top of the hamper.

What was the black thing, I wondered. I got off the toilet and went over to the hamper. It was a mini tape-recorder. When checking the bathroom earlier I didn't remember seeing it there. A pink Post-it note was stuck to the recorder, with the words—Listen Up!—written on it. I felt like Alice after she had found the Eat Me cake.

Just curious, I told myself, and pocketed the recorder. Then I slipped out of the apartment, undetected by Anna.

IV

When I got back to my apartment I took off my damp clothes and put on my flannel pajamas. I fixed myself a cup of Smoky Russian tea and sat in my recliner. Immediately, Keaton found my lap and curled up there. I clicked the PLAY button on the recorder. For about a half-a-minute, nothing, then Jimmy's voice came on.

Last night I had the dream again, except this time the television was suspended over my head. Otherwise, the dream was exactly the same. I am lying in bed, yet it's not my bed. I am in a hospital bed, though what makes it a hospital bed I'm not sure. The room does not possess the characteristics of a hospital room. No doctors or nurses come to check on me. There's nothing that visually indicates: You are in the hospital. Yet I feel strongly that I am in a hospital and that I am recovering from something. That I have been in recovery, in this bed, for a long time.

The room is dark, and except for the bed, I believe it's empty. Until the television turns on. A bright blue screen.

The television, in the first dream, was mounted on the wall, directly opposite my bed. The screen stays blue for what feels like a long time, then there is a high-pitched frequency and a series of multi-colored bars monopolize the screen. They are quickly displaced by a dignified-looking man who is sitting behind a desk, his hands neatly folded. He is wearing old-fashioned spectacles and his beard is neatly cropped. The thick gold ring on his finger demands my attention. He speaks in a serious yet friendly voice: Uninspired and luckless? Ghostwriters, Inc. will help you get on track. You know what your dreams are, your ambitions, you understand that your personal destiny is at stake. So do we.

Then the TV goes black and the room suddenly fills with the overpowering scent of flowers. That's when I wake up, agitated.

In the second dream, when the TV is suspended over my head, its screen facing down, I have a terrible sense that at any second it's going to fall and crush my head. When I woke up from that dream, I was not only agitated, but scared.

I clicked off the recorder. I felt queasy. The first agitated wasn't so bad, but the second one, which too quickly followed the first, had gotten to me. I have this thing, what you might call a word-allergy. Certain words, when I hear them spoken aloud, make me feel sick. I've had this condition ever since I was a kid. There are varying degrees to how sick I feel, depending on the word, and other circumstances. Like how many words throughout the day have already made me ill. Or if a variety of "trigger" words come at me in a stream or cluster. Typical effects are light-headedness and nausea. Sometimes I break out in a rash. Fortunately, it is only these trigger words spoken aloud, and not read or written, that make me ill.

I went to the fridge and poured myself a glass of club soda. I squeezed lemon into it. I drank it down quickly and burped. My stomach began to settle.

I went back to the recliner to resume listening to the tape when the phone rang. I picked it up.

Yell-oh, I said.

Mellow, came the response.

It was Tania.

Hey, T, how's it going?

Can't complain.

Still at your Ma's?

Yea, still here.

How's she doing?

On the mend, you know.

Tania's mom had broken her hip and Tania had moved in to take care of her.

What have you been up to, Sal?

Nothing much.

What are you doing for work?

Me? I'm deadpanning for pennies.

Oooohh, funny money.

That's what I most cherished about Tania: she was not one to miss a beat.

Tania turned on a hoity-toity British accent and said: I was calling to see if you would honor me with the privilege of your esteemed company this Friday.

For?

A modern dance interpretation of The Snow Queen.

Tania's voice returned to normal and said: I got two free tickets from a co-worker. What do you say?

I say count me in.

Great.

Chinese first?

Sure.

The Golden Dragon?

Perfect.

You are capital, Mr. Lunzezzi. Five o'clock at the Dragon, okay?

See ya then, T.

I hung up the phone, my stomach now fully stabilized. Tania was a lot better than club soda when it came to making me well. She and I had met in junior high and had dated briefly when we were in high school. After high school, I left to travel and when I returned we once again got romantically involved. We dated for several years, and had even talked about marriage. Yet a lot of what made us great as friends didn't translate to us as a couple. So we split up, didn't talk for about a year, eventually re-discovered the charm of our connection and have been friends ever since.

I went back to the couch and sat down. Keaton remained asleep by my side. I hit the PLAY button. There was a brief stretch of dead air, then Jimmy came back on.

When I saw the commercial on television, in real life, I wasn't surprised. Or I should say I wasn't as surprised as I probably should have been. The commercial wasn't the same commercial though. The man promoting Ghostwriters, Inc. was not the dignified-looking man from my dream. It was a younger man with sandy-colored hair and a handsome face. His chin looked strong and his eyes were astonishingly blue. What was the same: he wore a thick gold ring which demanded my attention. He introduced himself as Howell Downs, the founder and president of Ghostwriters, Inc.

The words he spoke were also different from the words in the dream. His message started the same—Uninspired and luckless?—then went on—Ghostwriters, Inc. just might be your salvation. It is quite common for writers to go dry, to lose their inspiration, to have their connection with the Muse compromised. If you know it's somewhere inside you and are struggling to get it out, there's no shame in saying: I need some help.

Howell Downs went on some more but I tuned him out. I didn't need to hear anything else. Before the real commercial, even before the dream commercial, I understood that something was about to change in my life. I didn't know how or what form it would take, but the funny thing was: I had written those exact words—uninspired and luckless—in regards to myself. Maybe that's why the commercial's appearance in real life didn't surprise me. All of it made perfect sense.

Silence followed. I waited for Jimmy's voice to return. It didn't. What I heard next was the sound of moaning. It was low, muffled. It didn't sound sexual. It sounded like the moan of someone who might be sick. Or having a nightmare. The moaning went on for a short while then stopped. There was about thirty seconds of silence before Jimmy's voice came back on.

Laura Ciccerone's Nightstand. A story by James Barrone.

Jimmy's words were followed by what sounded like him, or someone else, drinking from a glass. Then Side A of the tape clicked to an end. I decided to take things slowly and not play Side B until I felt ready.

I hadn't heard the name Laura Ciccerone in a long time. She was mine and Jimmy's classmate from 1st through 5th grade. Laura was petite, with short brown hair and a pretty face. She had big eyes and wore glasses. Jimmy had a profound crush on Laura, yet he never asked her out or made his feelings known. What Jimmy did do: he cast Laura as a character in every one of his stories.

In grade school, Jimmy's nickname was Dickens. He'd write story after story, casting us, his classmates, in different roles. Whenever Jimmy finished a new story it would circulate around the classroom. We were always eager to see who or what Jimmy had turned us into. Jimmy also played matchmaker. He'd have Frankie dating Toni Ann in one story, and Jerry dating Trish in another.

Even though Jimmy was always the main character, the hero in every story, he never paired himself up with Laura. She was always someone else's girlfriend. I didn't know if he did this to throw Laura off-track in regards to his feelings for her or if there was some other reason. In one story, Jimmy paired me up with Laura, about which I had mixed feelings. I was happy to have the always smiling and pretty Laura Ciccerone as my girlfriend, even if for only one story, but I knew how much Jimmy liked Laura and felt bad about making time with his girl.

Laura Ciccerone eventually went to a different junior high than Jimmy and me, after which we didn't see much of her anymore. Still, Jimmy kept putting Laura in his stories, now splitting her up into different characters with different names. Laura Ciccerone became Denise Martinelli, Jenny Rinaldo, Rosemarie Boccacio, Daniella Parisi, Sandy Marino. Jimmy never stated outright that these girls were Laura Ciccerone or re-imagined facsimiles of her, but I knew.

Years later I bumped into a grade-school classmate, Tommy Riley, and we decided to have a cup of coffee together and shoot the historical breeze. At one point in the conversation Laura's name came up and Tommy said—She was a cutie. I think we all had a crush on her, huh? I heard she lives in North Carolina now.

And that was the last time I had heard the name Laura Ciccerone. Until tonight.

I took out my little black notebook and wrote: Ghostwriters, Inc. Beneath that I wrote: Howell Downs. I put my notebook away and clicked on the TV, on the miraculous off-chance that I'd see the commercial.

The TV was selling cars, pizza, panty-hose, movies, appliances, heart medicine, facial crème, jeans, video games, perfume, diuretics. Pretty much everything except writer's inspiration.

I clicked off the TV and went to the bathroom, where I flossed, brushed and gargled. I decided to listen to Side B of the tape tomorrow, after I had chance to dream over everything that had happened today.

V

The next morning when I woke up I tried to recall any strange or prophetic-seeming dreams. Nothing. It's like I'd slept in utter blankness and had brought the blankness with me into my waking life.

I fixed myself coffee and scrambled eggs. Then I fixed Keaton's breakfast: moist Nine-Lives mixed in with a bit of warm milk. I went out into the hallway and swiped my neighbor's Daily News. The headline read: East Brooklyn Bloodbath. Something about a shooting in a convenience store.

I turned to the sports section and went through all the basketball boxscores. I liked to imagine the games in my head. I'd sketch in all the dramatic action based on individual and team statistics. The Knicks had gotten drubbed by the Rockets, 116-97. The game in my head wasn't a pretty one for the Knicks: too many turnovers, miscues and defensive breakdowns.

After my second cup of coffee I was ready to listen to Side B of the tape. I settled in my recliner and clicked on the recorder.

Jimmy's voice:

Today my ParaNormalizer will come over and perform the channeling. I am wondering what kind of ghost I will get? What will it feel like inside me? And the writing, what will that be like?

Fifteen seconds of dead air. Then:

My ParaNormalizer was a woman named Claire. She was very serene, very gentle. None of her movements were hurried or performed out of sync. The ritual had the makings of a séance: candles, quiet, concentration. When Claire was done she said a path had been successfully cleared and my ghost should arrive within the next two to twelve hours.

Exact arrival time is impossible to know, Claire said, and gave me a big smile. I didn't want Claire to go. I knew the relaxing effect she had on me would wear off as soon as she left. I asked Claire if she would like a cup of tea or something else to drink, but she said she had other appointments. I thanked Claire and watched her leave. Instantly I felt sad. Then I thought about how my ghost would be arriving soon and I perked up.

I clicked off the tape and wrote down the name Claire in my little black notebook.

I clicked the tape back on.

Ten seconds of dead air. Then:

It wasn't how I expected it to happen. I was on the couch, reading a magazine, when I heard a crackling sound. Like Rice Krispies when you pour milk over them. I put down my magazine and sat up. The crackling sound was coming from several feet in front of me. I couldn't trace it to a source.

Then, very slowly, what looked like a luminous plasma bubble started to materialize. It was blue and large and round. By the time it finished materializing, some of its roundness had melted away and its blueness was now glaringly vivid. It hurt to look directly at it. I kept blinking and shuffling my eyes away, then back, away, then back.

Hello, I said.

A voice came to me in stereo-effect.

Hello, it said back, and the word hello echoed at high-speed, as if spoken by many voices.

Are you my ghost, I asked it.

Yes, it responded, and this time the voice was more concentrated and less amplified. I stared at the ghost, which now looked more like an egg than a bubble. An egg that stood about five feet tall. It pulsed and flashed, as if it might go out at any second.

What now, I said.

We get acquainted, it said, its voice now a fully concentrated monotone.

May I, the ghost asked me.

May you what, I said.

Enter, it said.

He means me, I thought. It must have sensed my uneasiness because it said—Just to make sure I can. Some beings, whether consciously or unconsciously, reject entries. Others require a lot of time and patience before they can accept and hold entries. Then there are the ones who take to it right away. I want to know which kind you are.

It was weird. Though the ghost had no features or distinctive characteristics, I could feel it smiling.

Okay, I said, and took several deep breaths.

When it entered me it felt like my entire body had been hit with the flu. A flu that was packed in cold mud.

I let the tape play until the end but there was nothing else. I put the tape recorder in the top drawer of my desk. What now, I thought.

A tiny voice of logic was quick to respond—You should look for a job. One that pays.

That voice was tiny, therefore easy to ignore. A more prominent voice spoke next—You've still got a couple of weeks before the rent is due. Money always turns up one way or another. Don't worry about it.

That voice I liked and listened to, as it piped up again, loud and commanding—Curiosity might not pay your bills, Salvo, but it's got you in its grip. There's no turning back now. You're on the case.

I appreciated that the voice had used the word case, making it sound official. It, the voice, knew how to phrase things, words of seduction, words that slipped in warmly.

I took a white envelope out of my desk drawer. I counted

the bills inside of it: Two hundred and twelve dollars. I placed two twenties and a ten in my wallet and put the rest back in the envelope.

I called information and asked for the number for Ghostwriters, Inc. The operator gave me the number, which I dialed. A woman answered. I asked her where they were located. She gave me the address, which I wrote in my little black notebook, then hung up.

I made two turkey and cheese sandwiches and wrapped them in foil. I stuffed one in the left pocket of my coat, one in the right. Then I left, returning my neighbor's Daily News on the way out.

VI

I took the R train to Times Square and made my way through the glut of tourists, en route to Ghostwriters, Inc. They were located in a building on 41st street, between 9th and 10th.

In the lobby of the building I signed in, then took the elevator to the seventh floor. The elevator door opened directly into the lobby of Ghostwriters, Inc.

The lobby was a box-shaped room with chairs lining the walls and potted plants taking up the corners. Several of the chairs were occupied by men, writers I presumed. They briefly looked in my direction when I stepped out of the elevator, then quickly went back to whatever it was they were respectively absorbed in.

I went to the reception desk and said—I'd like to see Mr. Howell Downs.

Without raising her eyes from her paperwork, the receptionist handed me a ledger with a document attached to it, and in a nasal twang said—Fill this out and bring it back to me when you're done. The receptionist punctuated her command by loudly clacking the gum she was chewing.

I took the ledger and sat down. Aside from the usual requests—Name, Phone Number, Address, Date of Birth—there were questions like:

What are your reasons for enlisting the aid of a ghost?
In what genres do you feel your greatest aptitudes lie?
What is your publishing history, if any?
Do you have any specific goal(s) you would like to accomplish while partnering with your ghost?

I tried to imagine myself as Jimmy, and how he might have responded to these questions. Then I wrote in answers, allowing my hand to be guided by instinct.

There was an extensive checklist pertaining to physical and mental health background. I scored 100, not checking off a single box. When they asked if I had any allergies, I left it blank, not wanting to have to explain the word thing.

I finished the paperwork and handed it in to the receptionist. Wait until your name is called, she said, to the soundtrack of gum-chewing.

I sat down and waited. I found myself drawn to the hands of the man sitting directly opposite me. He was a blade-faced older man and his hands, which were set in his lap, twitched out a staccato rhythm. The twitching made me want to clap my hands or stomp my feet. Or scream. Instead I took one of the turkey and cheese sandwiches out of my coat-pocket and focused on every bite as I slowly ate it.

When I finished the sandwich, I picked up a Cosmo from the coffee table in the center of the lobby. After taking one of its quizzes, I found out that I was lonely, frustrated and in need of an affirmative outlet. Since the quiz was intended for women, I disregarded the results. I moved on to other magazines.

Two-and-a-half magazines later, my name was called.

Salvatore Massimo Lunezzi, paged the nasal twang.

I rose to my feet and the receptionist guided me to an office at the end of a long hallway.

Go right in, the receptionist said, then went back to her post.

I entered to a man wheezing and coughing into a yellow handkerchief. He kept trying to speak, but whatever attack he was having kept drawing him back to the handkerchief. He gestured with his free hand for me to sit down. I sat.

The man behind the desk was not the man Jimmy had described on the tape. Not the man from the real commercial, nor the man from the dream commercial. The man behind the desk wore horn-rimmed glasses and the whites of his eyes were flooded pink. He was balding, with clouds of salt-and-pepper hair puffing out the sides of his head like starched wool. With the handkerchief covering half his face, he looked like an accountant turned addict turned bank robber.

After an emphatic blowing of his nose, he stuffed the handkerchief back into the breast-pocket of his suit-jacket, adjusted his glasses, and said—Something about this office. Asbestos, toxins, bad mojo. I don't know what it is, but it gets in me and I'm wrecked.

The man smiled, but not enough that I could tell if the office comment had been an attempt at humor or a confession.

Are you Howell Downs, I asked him.

No, no, no, he clucked. I'm Arnold J. Kornish.

He then verified his claim by tapping his forefinger against the rectangular plaque on his desk, which read—Arnold J. Kornish.

Kornish pressed down on a plastic pump, sanitized his hands, then stood up and extended a dead fish of a hand for me to shake, which I did. He sat back down and said: So, Mr.—his eyes scanned the sheet in front of him—Lunezzi. Did I say that right? Loo-nay-see.

Yes, but you can call me Sal.

Very good. So, Sal, you're in the market for a ghost, I gather?

Possibly, I said, but I would like to meet with Mr. Howell Downs before I make any decisions.

Kornish smiled, his upper lip curling as if it had been stung by a bee.

You and many other people would love to meet with Mr. Downs, Kornish said, but that's a very difficult thing to make happen. You see, Ghostwriters, Inc. is just one of nearly two-dozen businesses that are owned by Mr. Downs. His entrepreneurial savvy keeps him on the go and virtually impossible to pin down.

What I can assure you though, Kornish continued, is that the spirit of Ghostwriters, Inc.—if you'll pardon the pun—as cultivated by Mr. Downs, is maintained at the highest possible level.

Kornish smiled his bee-sting-smile again. The horn-rimmed glasses made his eyes look swimmingly big, especially in relation to the rest of his features, which seemed shrunken and tightly drawn together. All except his nose, which began modestly, then grew longer and wider as it moved out toward the tip, as if it were reaching for something just out of reach.

Okay, Mr. Kornish, I said. I guess my destiny is in your hands.

Right-o, he cheerily agreed. Then he held up a finger—Just give me a moment to quickly review your paperwork.

Kornish perused my paperwork, mumbling bits and pieces of what I had written under his breath. When he was done he looked up at me and said—So there's a novel you've been working on for years?

Yes, I lied.

Kornish looked down at the paperwork again.

Laura Ciccerone's Nightstand, he said.

That's the one.

What's it about, he asked with what seemed like genuine curiosity and not just professional courtesy.

It's hard for me to put it into words, I said.

Perhaps that explains your block, Kornish cracked, and chuckled good-naturedly.

I echoed his chuckle. I imagine he took this as a sign of our burgeoning rapport.

When was the last time you worked on your novel, Kornish asked.

Let me think ... maybe nine, ten months ago.

I see, Kornish said, and paused, adding gravity to his next question—And completing this novel is important to you?

I also took a gravity-pause before responding—Probably the most important thing in my life, Mr. Kornish.

Kornish looked at me and nodded—slowly, reverently. No words, just this nodding which seemed to sanctify my plight and existence as a writer.

All of a sudden something definite clicked inside me. I

wasn't a man pretending to be a writer struggling to complete a novel. I was a writer struggling to complete a novel. Was this what actors experienced, I wondered.

I must have appeared distracted, because Kornish said—Sal, you still with me?

The grotesque beauty that was Kornish's nose came back into focus.

Yes, yes, I said. I was just ... thinking about the novel.

I can tell that it means a lot to you, Sal, which is why Ghostwriters, Inc., may provide the salvation you're seeking.

Kornish's voice came across canned and quasi-Biblical. Creamed corn at The Last Supper.

I studied his hands, which were now set on the desk, fingers neatly twined. The ring that Kornish was wearing was not a thick gold one that demanded my attention, but rather a simple silver band, set with a dark knuckle of a gem. As if aware that I was studying his hands, Kornish slid them out of view.

How did you hear about us, Kornish asked me.

Through a friend.

Kornish nodded. And how much do you know about the ghosting process?

Not much.

Kornish opened a drawer and took out several glossy brochures, and what looked like an instruction manual. He handed them to me.

This material will provide you with a general overview of who we are and what we do. Did your friend explain to you how the ritual is conducted by what we call a ParaNormalizer?

Yes, I said. In fact, I wanted to ask you about one of your ParaNormalizers, a woman named Claire.

Claire, Kornish said vacantly, his eyes rolling to an unspecified point on the ceiling. Claire, Claire, Claire, he repeated softly, as if trying to summon an image of the woman belonging to that name.

I'm not sure I know who you're talking about, he said. I

must confess that I don't quite know the names of all the ParaNormalizers in our employ. She might be one of the new girls. What does she look like?

I don't know, I said. I just know that she's very serene, very gentle. And she doesn't hurry her movements or perform them out of sync.

Kornish gave me a quizzical look, then chuckled and said—I'd like to think that description could be applied to most of our ParaNormalizers.

Smiling, Kornish asked—Any other questions, Sal?

Let me think, I said, and let my eyes glide lazily across his desk. A picture of a wife. A paper weight. A letter opener. A blue-barreled Parker pen. After a brief pause, I asked: How does payment work, Mr. Kornish?

Ah yes, the Almighty American dollar and its place in the grand scheme of things, Kornish said with playful relish, slapping his hands against the edge of his desk. We offer a variety of plans, Sal. Our goal is to accommodate both the creative needs of our clients and their financial capabilities. If you will, Kornish said, and produced another glossy brochure.

Kornish went over the variety of plans, explaining the specific benefits that came with each. Ghosting could be purchased in blocks. Three months, six months, nine months, a year. There was also ghost-on-demand, which provided shorter spells of ghosting.

Most of the writers who sign up with us, Kornish explained, do so with a primary goal in mind. A novel, a play, a collection of stories. And these things usually require blocks of time. That being said, there are many X-factors: the work-habits and discipline of each writer, how strong their chemistry and partnership is with their ghost, their level of expectations, etc., etc.

I nodded, looked down again at the brochure in my hand, then looked up at Kornish—Okay, I'll have to think everything over.

Do that, Sal, Kornish said, lurching forward with vigor. That's exactly what I want you to do. Ghosting is not for everyone and because it is such a—well, esoteric means to an ambitious end—as Mr. Downs has stated, it is something that generates food for thought, and perhaps apprehension.

It hit me in the face first, then the stomach. I felt the overwhelming urge to puke, but tightened my throat and clenched my jaw. I tried to regulate my breathing.

Sal, are you okay? Kornish shot out of his seat.

Yea, I think something I ate has come back to haunt me.

There's a restroom at the end of the hall. On your left.

In the restroom I splashed my face with cold water. Then I cupped my hands together and scooped cold water down my throat. I brushed my teeth until the bristles turned pink with blood. I spit pink saliva into the sink, rinsed off my toothbrush and put my toothbrush and toothpaste away.

The word apprehension had detonated a nausea-bomb. What had made the explosion even worse was Kornish's use of perhaps right before apprehension. Perhaps apprehension. The haps in perhaps had conjoined with the app in apprehension, doubling the negative impact of the word apprehension.

When I got back to Kornish's office, he said, as if having rehearsed his lines while I was in the bathroom: You know, Sal, maybe it wasn't bad food coming back to haunt you. Maybe it was the office that got to you. Asbestos, toxins, bad mojo.

Just look at me, Kornish said, and held up his hands, as if openly displaying himself as a prime example of a wrecked specimen.

I smiled politely.

Anyway, he went on in the voice of a teacher about to conclude his lesson, your ambitions, your personal destiny ... these things are your business. If you decide to make it our business as well, I'm confident that we can help you bring the big picture into focus.

When speaking the term big picture, Kornish used his hands to pantomime a large screen. This gesture threw me off.

Thank you for your time, Mr. Kornish, I said, and pantomimed a clock when speaking the word time. I now felt Kornish and I were back on equal ground. We shook hands and I left.

The weather turned quickly. It was the middle of November and the air quality had gone from sharp to carnivorous. On the Friday I was to meet Tania it started snowing in the morning. The forecast was calling for a storm.

I still hadn't heard from or had been able to reach Jimmy. I considered going to the police, yet something in me said this wasn't a matter for the police. Ghosts, writing, fractals, a mysterious woman who could dissect you with her eyes. This was bigger than the police.

I went to the window and stared out. The world outside seemed like the inside of a giant snow globe in the midst of a frenzied shaking. Fat, fuzzy snowflakes whirled and somersaulted. The streets and sidewalks were caked with whiteness. Even though it was a little before ten in the morning, the sky had the gauzy look of dusk.

I recalled the game Jimmy and I used to play when we were kids, after a big snow. Winter Burial. Jimmy had come up with the name and the game. The premise was simple: we would take turns burying each other in the snow and see which one of us could stay "buried alive" longer. We had to be completely submerged in the snow, not a trace of us exposed. Jimmy won every time, seemingly impervious to both the cold and fear of suffocation.

I fixed myself a cup of Smoky Russian and took down Jimmy's book from my bookshelf. It was a collection of stories titled Milking the Elephant, set in Coney Island at the turn of the century. A small press in Williamsburg had published the book about ten years earlier, and as far I knew it was the only book Jimmy had ever published. The cover featured a monochromatic image of Steeplechase Park after a fire had razed it to the ground. A sign, which extended like a wrinkled banner from the upper-left-hand corner of the book, read:

See the Ruins ... Only Ten Cents!

I opened the book and read the inscription, which Jimmy had written in his slurred handwriting:

To Salvo, Who Truly Understands That Life is a Great Curiosity, and Not a Quantifiable Formula ...

Love, your Brother from Another Mother-with-the-same-name, Jimmy

The mother-with-same-name comment had to do with the fact that both my mother and Jimmy's mother had been named Gabriella. I lay down on the couch and flipped to the story "Scale Model," which was my favorite in the collection. It was a love story about Carl, a chronic boozer who maintained and repaired the rides at Luna Park, and Winnie Lilliputian, who at thirty-six inches was billed as the smallest woman in the world, and worked at one of the freak shows on Coney Island's promenade.

There was a passage, unremarkable on the surface, which affected me more profoundly than any other passage in the book. It comes toward the end of the story, when Carl has gone to Lilliputian's apartment after a bender, which has cost him his job.

"He kneeled down, and she began, without looking at him, to straighten his shirt, fastidiously tugging on it just beneath the collar."

As was my custom, I re-read the passage over and over again, and let its secret power take hold of me. I felt sad, tender, broken, hopeful. Human.

I read a couple more stories before I dozed off.

I opened my eyes, or so I thought, and the light was blinding. My eyes adjusted quickly, as did my sense of location. I was walking on the beach, barefoot, and the sand was stinging-hot. To my left was Laura, to my right, Jimmy.

How about here, Laura said, indicating a spot where we could settle. Before Jimmy or I could answer, Laura spread her Marilyn Monroe beach towel on the sand and tossed the canvas bag she was carrying onto the towel. Jimmy spread his James Dean beach towel next to Laura's Marilyn Monroe. I didn't have an iconic beach towel, or even a regular beach towel for that matter. I sat on the edge of Jimmy's James Dean.

Laura was wearing a black one-piece bikini and wasn't wearing her glasses. The brightness of the sun set off the brown in her eyes, giving it a moist and rich quality. Jimmy and I were shirtless and in swim trunks.

It's nice for all of us to finally make it to the beach, Laura said, as if it were something we had been planning on for a long time. In the immediate distance reigned Astroland, and Laura chirped—We've got to go on the Cyclone before we leave. Jimmy agreed. I said nothing.

I used my hand to screen my eyes from the sun and stared out at the ocean. It was a choppy mixture of slate-gray and pale-green. The waves rolled in, ornery and hunchbacked, and hissed upon dispersion.

Jimmy sprang to his feet. I'm going in. Anyone care to join me?

Later, Laura said. After I bake in the sun for a while.

Salvo, Jimmy said.

I'll stay here and bake with Laura.

Jimmy flashed me a perverse smile as if I had meant something else by my remark. Had I meant something else by my remark?

Okay then, Jimmy said, I'm off to catch a mermaid. He bounded away toward the ocean.

Sal, will you do my back, Laura asked, and handed me a bottle of Coppertone lotion.

She lay flat on her stomach and unclasped the back of her bikini. I squeezed a glob of lotion into one hand, then rubbed both hands together and massaged the lotion into Laura's skin, starting with her shoulders. Laura's skin was warm, like bread just out of the oven. That warmth, combined with the coconut scent of the lotion, made me want to rest my head on Laura's back and fall asleep there. I worked my hands down to the base of her spine then stopped.

Thanks, she said, then asked—Do you want me to do you?

Sure, I said.

Laura re-clasped her bikini, then turned around and sat up. Her left cheek was pink and line-marked from having been pressed flat against the beach towel. I turned my back to Laura and her lotion-slick hands made circular patterns on my shoulders.

Do you think Jimmy will come back with a mermaid, Laura asked.

Probably, I said.

He's the type you know. And if he doesn't find one, he'll make her up. Like he did me.

I waited for Laura to say more. She didn't. Her silence was immediately followed by an absence of hands. Her touch was gone. My back and skin felt deprived, lonely. Then the rest of me did as well and I got a severe case of chills in what had to be 95° heat.

I turned around. Laura was gone. Marilyn Monroe was still there. As were Laura's canvas bag and the bottle of lotion, lying on its side.

Jimmy came back, his skin glistening with sea.

No mermaid, he said, smoothing his dark wet hair back with his hand.

She's gone, Jimmy, I said.

Who is, Jimmy said, standing over me.

Laura, I said. She was putting lotion on my back and then she just vanished.

Putting lotion on your back, eh, Jimmy said, with a crackle in his voice, and playfully kicked me in the shin.

Jimmy, she disappeared. Do you understand? Disappeared.

Too much sun on the brain, Jimmy said, and profusely tapped his finger against his temple. Look, he said, and pointed in the direction of the boardwalk.

I turned to look. Where, I said.

There, Jimmy said, and wagged his finger. It's Laura.

At first the heat obscured my vision, then I saw at whom Jimmy was pointing: a young woman in a cherry-red bikini, holding an ice cream cone, slowly walking in our direction.

Jimmy that's not Laura, I told him.

Not her, her, Jimmy said, and his finger zeroed in on a new target. A cocoa-skinned girl with ringlets of curls, leaning against the railing of the boardwalk. Not Laura.

I was struck mute and dumb. Jimmy sat down next to me, knees arched, hands resting on his kneecaps. He stared out toward the ocean and stayed quiet. I sensed that Laura the disappeared, Laura in the cherry-red bikini, Laura with the ringlets of curls—none of these Laura's were occupying his mind. He seemed to be waiting for something. Or someone. Then she came.

A young girl, maybe eight or nine, masked in wet goggles, fresh out of the sea. As she drew nearer to us, I saw Jimmy's eyes light up.

Thought you said she disappeared, Jimmy intoned facetiously. Then he punched me in the arm. The scene instantly dissolved in a blur.

I was staring up at the Z-shaped crack in my ceiling. I felt a weight on my chest. It was Keaton, poised there like an ominous Egyptian statue. I scanned the digital clock: 5:15. I cleared my chest of Keaton yet couldn't clear my head of the dream as I got ready for my date with Tania.

I got off the train at 34th street and found myself in another world. The snow hadn't let up all day, and its effect on the city was that of a morphine-fix for an organism used to running on steroids. The pace of traffic and activity were considerably slower. Sounds, usually blunt and high-volume, were softened and muffled by the snowy blanket unfurling across the streets and sidewalks. The snowstorm was superimposing an alien makeover onto the city and I felt giddily dislocated as I slowly made my way to 38th street, between 5th and Madison.

When I arrived at the Golden Dragon I saw Tania sitting at the end of the bar, chatting with Sam, the manager. Sam was a middle-aged Chinese man with thin jet-black hair that poofed several inches high off his scalp, a fastidious symmetry aligning each follicle. He was wearing his trademark white collared shirt and red jacket. Sam spotted me and gestured—Heyyy, look who's here!

I walked over and shook hands with Sam. Then I pecked Tania on the cheek. She rose from her stool and hugged me. I had forgotten how good it felt to be hugged by Tania. She put all of herself into her hugs, so you never felt cheated. We sat down and Sam said—It's really coming down out there, isn't it?

A regular winter wonderland, I said.

What are you drinking, Mr. Sal, Sam asked.

I looked over at Tania's drink. A martini.

How about a hot sake, I said.

How about it, Sam said with great cheer and went to prepare the sake.

How are you, Tania said, and gave my forearm a slight tug.

I'm good, I'm good.

She sipped her martini then went on—Any news to report?

On?

On anything.

Maybe.

Tania took my maybe and ran with it.

Oooh, a mystery. Who is she?

Who?

The mystery girl that's got your tongue on lockdown.

Before I could answer Sam returned with a small bottle of sake and a cup, which he poured the sake into. I sipped it slowly, enjoying the feel of its warmth on my lips and tongue.

So, Mr. Sal, Sam said, you don't come in here anymore. Why not?

I don't work across the street anymore.

I had been a porter in a building across the street for a couple of years. After work, a group of us who worked in the building would head over to the Golden Dragon for happy hour.

You quit, Sam asked.

Yea.

Why you quit?

I got tired of taking out people's trash, Mr. Sam.

Sam nodded. Where you working now?

He's deadpanning for pennies, Tania chimed in on beat.

Deadpanning for pennies, Sam said, curiosity raising his pitch. What is deadpanning for pennies?

It's Tania's unique way of saying that I am a bum, I said, and smiled in Tania's direction.

Not true, she quickly countered. It's my way of saying that he's a wonderfully odd human being.

Sam kept smiling, having no idea what the hell either one of us was talking about.

Well I wish you luck in whatever you do, Mr. Sal, Sam said, then—Excuse me—and he shuffled off to greet the new customers who'd sat down at the bar.

Tania drained the rest of her martini, then rose and said—I've got to tinkle, Mr. Sal, but when I get back—there she paused, laid her hand on my shoulder and leaned in close—I want to hear all about your mystery woman.

I watched Tania walk away. She was wearing a tight-fitting burgundy dress, which flatteringly showcased her shoulders and upper back. I noticed that Sam and several other men at the bar were visually magnetized to her ass, which looked like halved pears keeping a tick-tock rhythm.

I hadn't seen Tania in a while and her presence, as both a personality and a female, struck me as new and exciting. Tania was tall, with lively dark hair and a formidable mouth. The subtle slant at the corners of her eyes hinted at her Russian and Ukrainian background. She had been a ballet dancer for years, and while she didn't dance anymore, she still possessed a lithe and sturdy body.

Tania was a fanatic when it came to eyewear and never owned less than six pairs of glasses at a time, always designer names. Tonight she was wearing angular, tortoiseshell Calvin Kleins.

When she got back I complimented her on her dress.

Thank you for the compliment, Salvatore, Tania said. I'm surprised I was still able to fit into this dress with all the weight I've put on.

Tania was mercilessly self-critical when it came not only to her weight but her physical appearance in general. She was too fat, her breasts were too small, her teeth too large. Then there was the matter of her left eye, which was off by a tick. She regarded this as an unsavory defect, while I found it to be a point of intrigue and arousal, and the thing which originally most attracted me to her.

Tania ordered another martini and seemed to have forgotten about her intent to question me about the "mystery woman," as she said—Tonight, Mister-deadpan-for-pennies, drinks and dinner are on me.

I will graciously accept your offer and not put up a fight.

You are a gentleman among Philistines, Tania said in a mock-scholarly voice. Then—Do you know what happened to me today?

What?

I was promoted to district manager.

Congratulations, Ms. Petrovavich, I said and clinked my sake cup against her martini glass.

Tania was a store manager at a high-end shoe store in midtown.

Does this mean you are now fully committed to the world of footwear?

I don't know what it means, Tania said in an uncertain voice. Then her voice grew solid—More responsibility and more money is what it means.

We decided to eat dinner at the bar. Tania drank a couple of more martinis and expansively detailed the ups, downs and sideways of living with and caring for her mother.

She closed with—I love her to death, Sal, I really do, and I'm glad that I can be there for her, but I can't wait to move back into my own place.

Tania rented a studio in the East Village, which she was presently subletting.

When we were done we walked arm in arm to 37th and 8th, where the theater was located. It was a black box which seated about seventy-five. When the lights came up, the stage was bathed in a cool blue light with smoky hints of rose. A haunting flute came over the P.A., and the woman dancing the part of Gerta, dressed in a bright yellow leotard, fluttered onto the stage like a stray leaf.

The show lasted a little over an hour, and several times I had snuck glances at Tania and saw her crying. Her tears added another layer of poignancy to the experience, and when the show was over I felt quiet inside. Tania rose to her feet, with many others, and boisterously applauded. She sat down and turned to me—Wasn't the woman who danced the part of the Snow Queen amazing?

She was, I said.

She choreographed the show. Her name is Angela Evans. When I watch someone like her, those are the times that I really miss dancing.

Yea but you're the district manager of a high-end shoe store, I cracked, but my attempt at humor fell flat.

Yea, was all Tania said. A small, deflated yea.

Do you want to go somewhere for a drink, I suggested.

Yea, said Tania, though this time it was resoundingly affirmative.

When we got outside, there she was. As if out of a winter's dream, with her bone-white face and night-forest hair intensified by the snowfall.

Anna, I said.

Good evening, Salvo. Funny running into you here.

Were you at the show, I asked her.

Yes, I arrived late. Wasn't it just beautiful, she said, and tapped my chest with her gloved hand.

Anna shifted her gaze to Tania, a quick scan of her existence, then back to me, and smiled.

I'm Tania, Tania said, and stepped forward.

Pleased to meet you, Tania, I'm Anna.

Anna extended her hand for Tania to shake, and once again the length of Anna's extraordinary fingers commanded my gaze.

Why did you run out on me the other night, Anna said in an even voice. No hostility or malice—a deadpan bordering on mischief.

I had to go. Something came up and I had to go.

Anna smiled a no-hard-feelings smile.

Well we should get together again. On Jimmy's behalf.

I nodded. I then expected Anna to give me her number or to ask me for mine, but she did neither.

Nice to meet you, Tania, Anna said, and smiled warmly.

Likewise, Tania said and nodded.

You two have a splendid night, Anna said, then turned and walked away.

As Tania and I made our way to 7th avenue, Tania said— The mystery woman is a mystery no more. And she's stunningly gorgeous.

Yea, I agreed.

But do you really believe it's a coincidence that you both showed up at The Snow Queen on the same night?

Maybe, I said.

Maybe not, Tania said, emphasizing not. This woman followed you, Sal. Which means: She might be the type you wind up marrying, or she might be the type you wind up taking out a restraining order against. Which do you think she is, Tania said, smiling big.

It's not what you think, I said.

Oh no? Why did you run out on me the other night, Salvo, Tania said, mimicking Anna's voice. What's that all about?

I don't know, I said. I really don't know.

Walking home from the train station, I had a vague suspicion I was being followed. Or maybe I was hoping I was being followed.

When I got to my apartment building I stood in the doorway, poised and expectant, waiting for my pursuer, imaginary or not, to add a fresh wrinkle to my life. When this didn't happen I shifted my attention to the lazily fluttering snowflakes, which were tinged a moist electric blue. This blueness extended itself to the upper crust of the snowfall on the sidewalk, and when seen beneath the amber tint of a streetlamp, there was a grainy, almost archival quality to it, as if I were looking at an old photo of snow, circa 1933.

Once I was in my apartment and comfortably settled in, I clicked on the TV and got lucky.

A & E was airing a documentary on the twilight years of Charlie Chaplin, after he had been branded a communist sympathizer by the U.S. government and barred from the country. Chaplin and his family eventually took refuge in Vevey, Switzerland, where he spent the last twenty-five years of his life.

There was a segment about how, after Chaplin's death, his body had been dug up from the cemetery by two grave robbers, who demanded a ransom from Charlie's widow, Oona. Oona refused to pay, saying her husband never would have approved of such a ridiculous exchange. Five weeks later, the police arrested two auto mechanics—Roman Wardas of Poland and Gantscho Ganev of Bulgaria—and both men were convicted of grave robbing and extortion.

I was perversely inspired by the fact that a life of slapstick had followed Chaplin beyond the grave. I tried to share my enthusiasm with Keaton, but perhaps because of his namesake he was thoroughly indifferent.

When the documentary finished I clicked off the TV, went to the window, and looked out.

Blue snow.

1933.

I didn't want normalcy to return anytime soon.

VIII

For the next several days Anna dominated my musings. Jimmy, Tania, Laura Ciccerone, ghosts—they all became specks in the background. I knew Anna would find me when she wanted to and the prospect of seeing her again made me feel sick with pleasure. And it wasn't a sexual thing. Maybe a part of it was but only a minor part. Or rather, a symptomatic side-effect to Anna's profound magnetism.

How could I explain it? I was drawn to Anna in the way that a small boy is drawn to his mother. A small boy who is still under the impression that he and his mother are the same being. No separateness, a soul-twinned intimacy.

That night when Anna had undone me with her eyes, I had wanted to drop to my knees and confess. What I confessed didn't seem nearly as important as the act of confession itself, and that Anna would be the one receiving my confession. Where had Jimmy and Anna met, I wondered. Were they really just friends or was there something more going on?

I had liked that Tania had called Anna stunningly gorgeous. It was like an expert jeweler appraising the value of a rare jewel. I also liked to think about Tania thinking about me and Anna as an item. Was Tania jealous of me and Anna? Was I jealous of Jimmy and Anna?

As my thoughts began taking soap-operatic turns, I realized I had spent too much time on the couch. I got up and did some stretches. Then I did fifty push-ups and ended with a prolonged headstand. When I was right-side-up again I checked the fridge. Slim pickings.

I scrambled my last two eggs then melted a slice of yellow American cheese on white bread and made a sandwich. I brewed coffee. The small amount of milk I had left had gone sour so I drank the coffee black. I poured the sour milk into Keaton's bowl. He instantly padded over and began lapping it up.

Waste not want not, eh buddy, I said to him, but he paid me no mind and kept at the drink.

Thanks to Tania my rent was paid. She had insisted on loaning me the money and said I could pay her back whenever. Whenever was a timeline I knew I could manage, so I felt okay saying yes. Still, I needed money. Not just for groceries and other living expenses but for ghosting. I had decided to try it at least once and see what it was like.

I sat down at the kitchen table and tried to think of ways to make money without working a regular job. I was through with regular jobs, at least for a while anyway. I was on my second cup of coffee when the light bulb clicked on. Rico Gonzalez.

Rico was a childhood friend of mine and Jimmy's who had grown up around the block from us. Rico was a hustler through and through. One of his regular gigs was a tag-switch scam. Rico would go to different clothing or department stores and switch the tags on merchandise, so a $750 coat became a $300 coat. Next, Rico, or whoever was his accomplice, would purchase the tag-switched merchandise, which would later be returned. When the returned merchandise was scanned, Rico would get store credit for whatever it had originally been worth. So the $750 coat purchased for $300 became a $750 coat again. Rico would then use store credit to purchase merchandise ordered by his clientele and sell it to them at a discounted price.

I called Rico and he picked up on the fourth ring. In the background I heard hip-hop music blaring and what sounded like his kids screaming.

Sal-eee-Baba, what's up, m'man, Rico boomed.

I was about to tell Rico what was up when he said—Hold on a sec, these kids are going crazy. Victor, he shouted, cut that shit out right now, right now, do ya hear me? If you make your sister cry one more time...

Rico let the threat hang and came back on the phone.

Wanna adopt a pain-in-the-ass five-year-old, Rico said.

No thanks, I have enough trouble taking care of a cat.

We reminisced about the old neighborhood for a short while, then I asked Rico if he needed any help with his tag-switch operation.

Operation, Rico laughed. You make it sound like I'm running a drug cartel or some shit. Anyway, YOU are in luck.

My luck had to do with the fact that Frankie, Rico's cousin and primary accomplice, had been in a car accident a while back and had just received a settlement for $100 000. Frankie's big payday meant he was taking a leave of absence from work and that his position was available.

Rico explained that I would get 25% of what he made, and that his business doubled during the holiday season.

When can I start, I asked him.

Tomorrow, Rico said. I'm driving to P.A. to hit a bunch of the outlet malls. I'll pick you up around nine. You still in Bay Ridge?

Yea, I said.

Ahrite, Rico said, then his voice broke away—Victor, WHAT DID I TELL YOU, WHAT DID I TELL YOU—I gotta go Sal, see ya tomorrow.

I hung up the phone feeling pretty good. I had a job. My rent was paid through the rest of the month. Anna could breeze back into my life at any moment. When she did, chances are I'd have money to invite her out for chocolate fondue or to see a revival of a silent film. She seemed like the type who would go for those sorts of things.

The next morning I waited outside my apartment building for Rico. It was a cold, overcast day with pockets of brightness straining to break through. The previous week's snowstorm had been followed by two days of rain and the ground was now a mess of gray slush.

Rico pulled up in his black Lexus a little after nine. I opened the passenger door and Biggie Smalls came blasting out. Biggie was one of Rico's heroes. Rico called Biggie the ghetto's black Sinatra.

Rico shouted over the music—Sal-fucking-eeeee—and gave me a shoulder-bump-hug. Rico was wearing a red-and-black Yankees cap, which matched his red-and-black Polo jacket. His eyes were hidden behind dark sunglasses. The car smelled strongly of whatever cologne he was wearing.

You ready to hustle up some Bennies, homeboy, Rico barked.

Business as usual, I said coolly, referring to the title of an EPMD album, which I imagined Rico would appreciate.

Sal-fucking-eeeee, Rico said again, then rapped a few lines from "Mr. Bozack," one of the songs on Business as Usual.

Rico reached into his pocket and produced a small white bottle. He popped the cap and shook a half-dozen pills into his palm. The pills came in two colors: white and pink.

Want any, he said.

What are they, I asked.

Klonopin and Percocet. Bring you to the relaxation tip.

I took several unsharpened pencils out of my coat-pocket and said—I've got these—and smiled.

Sal-fucking-eeee, still a crazy fucker aintcha, Rico laughed. He popped a pink and a white and washed them down with Evian. Biggie was rapping about smacking a bitch and stealing her Gucci bag as we drove off.

That day we hit several malls and everything went smoothly. Rico switched tags with a cool and quick efficiency, and I made purchases using the money that he gave me. By the end of the day, Rico had taken six pills and I had sharpened eighteen pencils. Driving back we ate Burger King and listened to Busta Rhymes. Busta's infectious, free-wheeling style made me want to throw a brick through somebody's window. Rico said he felt the same way.

Pennsylvania, Staten Island, Long Island, New Jersey, Manhattan, Brooklyn. The next two weeks were a furious whirlwind of purchases and returns, fast food and hip-hop.

Rico always did the tag-switching, and we both put in time making purchases. I handled most of the returns.

Rico had said, with great pride in his voice, that in all his years of tag-switching he had never been caught, not once. He had won every time.

How many people could say that? It was a rare and exceptional thing to stay undefeated, to remain perfect. Then there was the exhilarating high that it gave him. After we had completed a successful run, Rico's eyes and voice would be charged and I could feel the energy coming off him. It wasn't the same for me. Maybe because I wasn't the one switching tags. Or maybe because when I compared the effect it had on me with the effect that Anna had had on me, it felt second-rate.

During that two-week span, outside of hustling, not much else happened. I hadn't heard from Jimmy, nor had Anna magically re-appeared in my life. I'd heard from Tania, and one night we went out for drinks and to see the latest Woody Allen film. Tania's mother was functional again so Tania had moved back into her own place.

It was early December and another snowstorm was in the forecast. I had made enough money to pay for ghost-on-demand. I called Ghostwriters, Inc. and scheduled an appointment. I was first to take a physical with one of their doctors, then I would be assigned a ParaNormalizer.

When I next met with Kornish he wasn't wheezing and coughing into a handkerchief. There was a healthy glow to his pallor, which was further buoyed by the lemon-yellow tie with red polka dots that he was wearing.

You're looking well, I said.

Am I, he smiled. Either I've gotten used to this office or it's gotten used to me, he said and shot me a wink.

Then he asked about my stomach. Had it been food poisoning?

No, no, it was—I paused. Why not, I thought. Actually, Mr. Kornish, it was something you said.

Something I said, he responded with slight alarm.

I wrote down the words Perhaps Apprehension on a piece of paper and asked him not to speak the words aloud. Then I explained about my word allergy.

When I was done, Kornish said—Fascinating, truly fascinating. Never ever have I heard of such a thing. He took a thoughtful pause, then—I wonder if your writer's block is any way tied in to your word allergy?

Writer's block, I thought to myself, drawing a blank. Then it clicked—Yes, I was writing a novel, Laura Ciccerone's Nightstand.

Maybe, I said to Kornish, but I don't think so.

Kornish was excited to tell me that he had found my girl Claire—that's how he had put it, my girl Claire—and that she would be my ParaNormalizer. He also explained that ghost-on-demand would entitle me to three sessions that could be used at any time within a three-month period.

If any questions or concerns should arise during your ghosting process, Kornish said, we have a 24-hour hotline and the number is listed on our brochure.

Kornish rose and vigorously thrust his hand forward for me to shake, which I did. It was no longer just a dead fish, but also a petrified one.

Good luck, Sal, he said. I hope that novel gets finished and becomes a best-seller.

Me too, I said, and that was that.

While riding the elevator down, I looked over the card Kornish had given me. Claire would be coming to my apartment at 10am on Monday. It was Friday.

When I got outside it was snowing. Maybe that meant Anna would soon be paying me a visit. As if out of a winter's dream.

IX

Monday came. The weather pattern, as if caught in a loop, was in full repeat. Friday's snowstorm was followed by two days of rain. Slushville all over again.

A good day for contracting a ghost, I told myself as I sipped my coffee. I scanned the clock. 9:42. Claire would be arriving soon. I had been up since 7:15, my mind grazing on all things ghost. Hamlet's dad, the young blonde girl in Poltergeist announcing "They're here," Jacob Marley dragging his chains, Casper, Amityville, that séance we held in Jimmy's hallway when we were kids. It was Jimmy, me, and several of our friends and we tried to summon the spirit of Jimmy's dad, Nick, who had died from a heroin overdose when Jimmy was one. Except for our friend Peter's volcanic fart that caused the candle-flame to quiver, no other phantom force had made its presence felt during the séance.

I turned on the radio and tuned in to the jazz station. Billie Holiday was singing "In My Solitude." Her honey-slow voice worked its way inside me. I abstracted her voice into a weather pattern and myself into the weatherman announcing it: Warm with a slight chance for scabbing and Paris.

I looked in and saw myself slow-dancing with Tania, my hand in hers, our bodies grafted. We were in a cellar-lounge mood, thick with boozy trumpets and oily shadows. I suddenly had the overwhelming urge to call Tania and tell her who was coming over and what I was about to do. I hadn't told Tania about Jimmy's phone call, nor any of the curious things which had come into my life since. Things which were moving me, not necessarily forward, but maybe deeper inside or a splintered kind of sideways.

I picked up the phone and dialed Tania's work number. A woman with a sing-song voice answered and I asked to speak with Tania.

Sure, who's calling, the woman said, and that's when my doorbell rang.

Never mind, I said and hung up.

I checked the clock. 9:49. I thought it promising that my ParaNormalizer was arriving early in sloppy weather conditions. Rapping on the door. I opened it and there stood a pink-cheeked woman with a black bag slung over her shoulder.

Mr. Lunezzi, she said.

Sal, I said. Claire, right?

Yes.

We shook hands lightly and I invited her in.

Crazy weather we're having, huh, Claire said, as she peeled off her gloves then began unwinding her scarf.

Tell me about it, I said.

Keaton immediately gravitated to Claire's leg and performed a slow graceful orbit around it while nuzzling her calf.

Who is this sweetheart, Claire said, as she kneeled down and scratched the underside of Keaton's chin.

Keaton, I said.

Michael or Buster?

Buster.

That's perfect, Claire intoned with musical cheer, which suggested that she preferred Buster to Michael. Another promising sign.

Keaton remained still, eyes closed, his purring cartoonishly loud.

Claire kept at his chin for a bit, and when she stopped she explained to him—I've got work to do Mr. Keaton—then she rose to standing. Keaton stared up at her with a look of pitiful longing.

I picked him up, thumb-scratching his scalp, and asked Claire—Would you like coffee or tea or anything?

No thank you, Sal, I'm all set, Claire smiled.

I hd heard the term pleasant-looking used before to describe a person, but never had I met someone who so acutely epitomized pleasant-looking. Attractive, pretty, cute, plain, handsome—none of these terms were right for Claire. Claire was pleasant-looking. When I looked at her an easy, benign feeling came into my stomach.

Claire had short, feathery, wheat-colored hair, a round face, and kind eyes. She was dressed in a white blouse, blue denim jeans, and had been wearing brown boots, which she had taken off and left on the mat in the hallway. Her socks were navy-blue and looked warm.

We were in the living room, where Claire prepared the space for the ritual. I observed her in action and found that Jimmy, that literary sonofabitch, had nailed it: none of her movements were hurried or performed out-of-sync. They were all part of an effortless flow.

Claire explained that it would be best if I made the apartment as dark as possible. Except for the bedroom, the rest of the apartment was consolidated in one large room. I drew all the necessary curtains. When I was done I grabbed a handful of unsharpened pencils, and my pencil sharpener, and sat on the floor, opposite Claire. She was slotting six lean white candles into six holders that were extensions of the bronze bowl she had set on the floor. The candles formed a circular wall around the rim of the bowl. In the bowl itself, which ran about five inches deep, Claire placed flat, smooth-looking blue-gray stones, a dozen in all.

What are the stones for, I asked.

For dramatic effect, Claire said and smiled. No they're actually, well ... sort of like conductors. Having solid matter as a central base for the light creates a stronger pathway for the incorporeal to cross over into the corporeal.

I nodded and wondered why the words corporeal and incorporeal, which usually made me at least mildly ill, hadn't affected me. Was it because it was the pleasant-looking Claire who had spoken them?

Are you getting ready for your ghost, Claire said, noting my pencils with her gaze.

No, I laughed, this is just something that helps me ...

remain calm and focused.

These stones kind of work that way for me, Claire said, moving them around as if searching for the right sequential combination.

Are they special stones, I asked her, or are they ordinary ones?

Claire smiled. I don't know if there's really such a thing as an ordinary stone, Sal, but to answer your question: yes, they are special. The woman who gave them to me was like my second mother, my spiritual mother I guess you could call her. She said these twelve stones were a family and they had to stay together. She had faith that I would honor that and would find a good use for them. Or that they would find a good use for me.

I stared at the stones, half-expecting them to speak or sing or do something dramatic. They remained still and quiet. Ordinary-like.

There, Claire said, satisfied with the position of the stones. Then—Are you ready?

Sure, I said, and placed the sharpener and the pencil I had been sharpening on the floor.

Is it dark enough in here, I checked.

Yes it's fine.

So I just sit here with you and that's it?

Sit here with me, give me your hands, and I'll do the rest.

My mind went back to the séance we had held as kids. Why hadn't it worked? We had candles, we held hands. Maybe it was the lack of stones.

Claire began lighting the candles. As if sensing what was about to take place, Keaton exiled himself to the bathroom.

Animals, especially cats, Claire explained, are extremely sensitive to the world beyond ours. You never know how they're going to react to an incorporeal visitor.

There was that word again, incorporeal, and again no ill-effects.

Claire finished lighting the candles. She flicked the match into the ashtray which held my pencil shavings and said—Give me your hands.

I gave Claire my hands. Claire's palms were soft and warm and coated with a thin film of moisture.

Close your eyes, Sal, Claire gently commanded.

I closed my eyes.

We sat cross-legged, our knees nearly touching, eyes closed, fingers entwined, in silence—for what might have been two minutes, might have been ten. I waited for Claire to say something, to petition the spirit-world on my behalf, yet she stayed quiet. At one point I cracked an eye to see if anything strange or dramatic was happening with the candles or the stones. There wasn't. The candle-flames swayed subtly, the stones remained stone-like.

Was this going to be a dud of a séance just like the Nick Barrone one had been, I wondered. Then, a pang of bitterness as I realized that had been a free dud, this one had cost me. The voice of my Uncle Silvio came to me loud and incredulous—You paid how much to hold hands with a girl by candlelight? You're a real mamaluke, you know that?

Before I had a chance to defend myself against Uncle Silvio, I was sidetracked by a low steady humming coming from Claire's throat. Its vibrational energy quickly shifted to her hands, where it intensified, and surged through my fingertips. The sensation grew warmer and pricklier as it climbed my arms. By time it reached the top of my shoulders, both my arms felt as if they had gone to sleep and had been colonized by spiky tingles. And though the humming was still audible, it now seemed as if it were background noise coming from my neighbor's apartment on the other side of the wall.

I tried to open my eyes but couldn't. It felt as if they were sealed shut. And the blackness which came with my eyes being closed wasn't the usual blackness. It was shot through with faint patches of color. Red, gold, green, blue. At first everything was still, then the colors began to circulate at high-speed and melt into one another. The colors grew more vivid and stabbingly intense, a strobelight shooting quills. I tried to close the eyes inside my eyes, and this compressed the dimensions of the disco blackness but didn't shut it out.

Claire's voice cut in and rescued me. Sal, Sal, came her voice bright and steady. I found that I could now open my eyes and there was Claire's face, a blurred white grape. When my vision came into focus I saw that the grape was smiling and that it had freckles.

Did you have freckles when you got here, I asked Claire.

Ever since I was nine, Claire responded, sliding her finger up and down the bridge of her nose where most of the freckles were concentrated.

Are you okay, Claire asked.

Yea fine, I said, and noticed that the humming sound was still reverberating in my right ear, a sort of pesky tickle. I plugged my finger into my ear and tried to rub it out but couldn't.

Claire blew out the candles then collected her stones. Matter-of-factly, she stated—A pathway was successfully cleared. Your ghost should be here by tonight, at the latest tomorrow.

And if it doesn't show, I said.

It will, Claire responded confidently.

She rose to standing and I did the same.

A pleasure meeting you Sal, Claire said, and extended her hand. I noticed that Claire's hand when being shaken formally felt different than Claire's hand when being held in a séance. Now that the ritual was over, like Jimmy, I didn't want Claire to leave. I offered her coffee or tea or if she wanted I could make her a sandwich. Her response pretty much echoed the one she had given to Jimmy—No thank you Sal. I've got to get going. I have another appointment.

Claire said good-bye to Keaton, telling him to take good care of me, and when she was at the front door, raveling her scarf around her neck, I knew what I needed from her before she left.

Claire, before you leave, I said, can you do me a favor?

What, she said.

I hustled over to my desk, grabbed a pencil and scrap of

paper and wrote the words—Expunge, Affidavit, and Apprehension—on the paper. Then I went over to Claire and said—Would you read these words aloud?

While nine out of ten people would have asked why, Claire simply took the paper and read aloud in a crisp, schoolteacher's voice—Expunge. Affidavit. Apprehension.

The nausea-strike was swift and layered. I was shaken up but maintained my poise.

Anything else, Claire said, handing the paper back to me.

I shook my head.

After Claire had gone I went to the bathroom, prostrated myself before the toilet, and puked up everything that was inside me. When I was done puking I brushed my teeth several times and gargled mouthwash. Then I took a long shower, making sure it was hot enough to burn my skin. I came out of the shower a new man. Calm, detached, no more pesky tickle in my right ear. I fixed myself a cup of Smoky Russian and sat on the couch where Keaton joined me.

What do you think about this ghosting business, I asked him.

Keaton's response was to yawn and stretch out his front legs. Soon he was asleep.

I killed time watching TV, reading, sharpening pencils, daydreaming. I listened to a bunch of old jazz records. Just like that it was after eleven and I fell asleep watching a re-run of Cheers.

It was a crackling noise, what sounded like grease spitting in a frying pan, which woke me up. Still half-asleep I turned to the TV and saw Art Carney trying to teach Jackie Gleason how to play golf. It was one of my favorite episodes of The Honeymooners. I started to watch it when the crackling sound, which I had somehow become oblivious to, reclaimed my attention.

By the time the luminous blue bubble began to materialize I was on my feet and fully awake. I was ready to receive my ghost.

"As from a star I saw, coldly and separately, the
separateness of everything. I felt the wall of my skin: I am I.
That stone is a stone. My beautiful fusion with the things of
this world was over."
—Sylvia Plath

"In the end, everything is a gag."
—Charlie Chaplin

PART II.

WHO'S ON FIRST?

I

I am standing over myself: a runt-skinny kid lying flat on his stomach, right elbow hunched, the stubby pencil in his left hand ferociously scribbling on a piece of unlined white paper. The paper is set directly against pimply stone, so the kid's handwriting comes out jaggedy and warbled, as if his left hand were stutteringly drunk.

It is August, early afternoon, and the heat is a thick fuzzy animal big enough to smother all of Brooklyn. A voice snaps from the top step of the stoop—Done. You wanna hear?

The voice belongs to Jimmy, age eleven, and he is wagging several white pages in his hand.

Of course I want to hear, I think, and nine-year-old-me sets down his pencil and shifts to an attentive seated position, angling his head toward Jimmy, who is poised on the top step of the stoop.

It's called The Double Curse of Cross and Bones, Jimmy says, then smacks his lips together loudly several times before launching into the story, which begins: Two wasn't always Miller's unlucky number.

I am not only standing over but am also inside of nine-year-old-me, which means I can feel the zip and crackle that comes with being an audience to Jimmy's stories. There is something in Jimmy's voice, a buttery charge, and the way the words skate off his tongue in happy bunches and intimate clusters, which makes me yearn for my own special relationship with language. That is why I am out here, on Jimmy's stoop, scribbling stories, part of our everyday summertime ritual, same as stoopball, firefly-hunting and playing war in the park.

When Jimmy is done reading he quickly begins talking about something else, before I have a chance to comment on his story. This too is part of the ritual. I can feel how awkward

I am inside of myself, as if my body were a too-tight suit that causes me to fidget and squirm. That being said, Jimmy's story has somewhat taken me out of myself in a way that my own stories do not, and I hear myself say—You're a great writer Jimmy—to which Jimmy snappishly responds—Aw shaddap with that Salvo ... ready for some stoopball—and he produces a pink Spalding and bounces it on the stoopstep, rubber pecking stone.

To say that the scene dissolved would be inaccurate. The scene between Jimmy and nine-year-old-me continued to play out, but I, as a witness, had gone. I was now back in my apartment in Bay Ridge, late morning, December, staring vacantly at the open notebook laid out on my desk.

My mind suddenly shifted to the realization that this was my third session with my ghost, Y., and unless I purchased another block, my last. I had planned to space out my sessions over an extended period of time, yet after the first session, and all that it had unlocked, I couldn't help but use the other two right away.

I didn't know what ghosting felt like for others, nor the ways in which it changed them, but for me it felt like a high-impact acid trip. I could spend what felt like hours looking inside of and behind a single word, and specific words had become things of felt beauty. Wisteria, octave, innuendo, scallion, solvent, calliope, adagio. Then there was Scandinavia. I had developed an exquisite crush on the word Scandinavia. To write it meant to enter a space of complex nostalgia. Nostalgia for what was and what was not, nostalgia for the future, nostalgia for your own death, nostalgia for the people you were and the people you were not. Scandinavia, more than any other of the charmed words, had become a lighted peephole through which I spied other lighted peepholes. I was on the inside looking out at the inside looking out.

I opened my notebook and re-read the stray bits I had marked down about Scandinavia:

Scandinavia is comprised of Denmark, Norway and Sweden. Iceland and Finland are sometimes mistakenly referred to as part of Scandinavia, but they are not part of Scandinavia. They are, though, like Denmark, Norway and Sweden, Nordic countries.

LEGO was founded in Denmark. IKEA and H & M were founded in Sweden. Norway has the largest population of arctic reindeer herders.

Hans Christian Andersen was born in Odense, Denmark in 1805. His first fairy tale booklet was subtitled: "Fairy Tales Told for Children."

The Swedish pop music group ABBA formed in Stockholm in 1972. Their band name ABBA is also the name of a well-known fishing company in Sweden. The fishing company had the name ABBA before the pop music group did.

Knut Hamsun was born in Lom, Norway on August 5th, 1949. His debut novel Hunger describes a young writer's struggles with despair, poverty and madness. Stream-of-consciousness, interior monologues and fragmentation were techniques that he used in getting at what he called "the whisper of blood and the pleading of bone marrow." Later in life he became a Nazi sympathizer and this severely compromised his reputation.

In Scandinavian folklore the Mylings are the wandering souls of unbaptized children who are seeking a proper burial, and are known for jumping on the backs of the living and demanding to be carried to the graveyard. They are also called Utburd—"that which is taken outside"—which refers to the practice of abandoning unwanted children in the woods or some other remote area.

I closed my notebook and sat motionless at my desk for a long while, feeling flat and infirm.

Then, not able to put it off any longer, it was time to disengage my ghost, Y. While I didn't exactly squeeze Y. out of my ass, the effort that went into ejecting it from inside me was similar to the effort that one puts into trying to pass a turd while constipated. I stiffened my legs, clenched my hands, and the muscles in my face and neck tensed as I forced Y. out.

Achy and flush, I instantly became aware of my body as my own again. My eyes, which stung a little and felt as if they were coated in filmy gauze, took in what was now before me, hovering several inches off the floor. A uniform assembly of particles, the size of dimes, flickering a translucent blue. With measured synchronicity one particle would be drawn toward another particle, stopping right before they touched, then the two would separate, never further than five or six inches apart. The rhythm was a perfectly repeated breath made visible: expansion swelled Y. to a sphere, contraction slimmed it down to an oval.

How do you feel, I asked Y.

Cold, came the monotone response, which was as much in my head as it was outside of it.

You, Y. asked.

Tired, I said. Tired, flat and full of nothing.

Y. didn't say anything and since it was featureless there was no expression to read.

Can you explain to me about the cold, I asked Y.

There is no way to explain it, Y said. It's a cold beyond words. Beyond human comprehension.

It had been right after my first session when I asked Y. what it was that ghosts gained from helping writers write, what was in it for them, if anything.

Y. had said: The opportunity, even when it's brief, to inhabit a body and being gives us two very important things: A sense of home. And warmth. Ghosts suffer from terrible cold. I'm not talking about climate-cold that can be measured in degrees, nor am I talking about the lonely-cold that drives people mad. I'm talking about cold in the abstract, a cold that seeks form and with form comes warmth. Unless you're a ghost you can't feelize what I'm talking about.

(Feelize was a term that Y. used time and again in our conversations. Y. said that felt-realizations—feelizations—were one of the strongest and most complete ways of knowing something. Of "getting it.").

Over the course of the past four days there were other things to which Y. had enlightened me:

Even though ghosts don't remember who they were, who they had been in their previous incarnation, they still had specific memories, yet the memories were attached to feelings and sensations, not to names and history. Y.: "I can remember loving someone, deeply, can remember what it had done to me, what it had felt like. I can remember the thrill of kissing and holding and touching another being, but I couldn't tell you who that being was—their name, background, stuff like that."

All ghosts, as far as Y. knew, were nameless and genderless. They all went by one of three standard designations: X., Y. or Z.

Y. still had no idea if there was a heaven or hell or anything like that. Y.: "For all I know I'm in a suspended state of limbo waiting to receive word about my re-location. The thing is I have no clue if that word exists, or if there is a place where the cold is permanently kept out."

3-B.   Because a place like this remained both a mystery and a possibility, Y. prayed a lot.

Possessing living beings is not as easy as some might think. When I had asked Y. why it and other ghosts simply didn't satisfy their need for warmth and home by willfully taking over living beings, Y. said—"It's extremely difficult. Even if you do manage to possess another being against their will, the success rate for staying inside them for an extended period of time is very low. You have to understand—you are trying to inhabit a being that is already inhabited by a living spirit, one that belongs there. Unless that spirit and that being are open to receiving a ghost—which usually only happens when someone wants to be possessed by a ghost for personal reasons, in your case that would be writing—you are more or less locked out. There are some ghosts who will do anything in their power to break a person's spirit and take control of their being. Some even force themselves on sleeping women, or rather inside them with the hopes of planting a seed in the woman through which they'll be reborn. These type ghosts, though, are the exception and not the norm."

Well I guess that's it, I said to Y., letting him know that our time together was up.

Yes I know, Y. said, unless of course you purchase another block.

Even though there was no inflection in Y's voice, his words gave me the feeling that it was under contract with Ghostwriters, Inc., and one of the stipulations of the contract was—Make sure you soft-sell the client and promote our business.

You trying to hustle me into another block, I suggested, to which Y. responded—Not at all. There are a lot of writers and would-be writers out there that are in need of help. A shortage of host-bodies is not an issue at this particular juncture in time.

Particular juncture in time, I repeated in my head, then said aloud—What, we in a creative crisis or something?

Y. didn't respond. Just pulsed and flickered, pulsed and flickered. All rhythm, no sound.

The fade-away was quick and sudden. No good-bye, no last words—gone. I had been hoping for some sort of closure, seeing as this had been my first relationship with a ghost. Instead, I would have to come to terms with the lack on my own. Either that or pony up more dough for another go-round.

Because of ghosting I had taken the week off from tag-switching with Rico. I was down to about $90 and needed to get back to work immediately and hope for a profitable run. Trying to orient myself in regards to what day of the week it was, and the date, I checked the wall calendar over my desk. Friday, December 15th. Ten days before Christmas, which meant there were still plenty of tags to be switched and merchandise to be sold.

I poured myself a glass of club soda, added ice, then sat at my kitchen table and dialed Rico's number.

Hello, came the voice like a sudden shot.

Hey, Desiree, it's Sal. How ya doin?

Oh Sal hey ... hey Sal .

Desiree, who was Rico's wife, sounded out of sorts.

Bad time, I said.

You didn't hear, Desiree said.

Hear what?

Rico got locked up. Dumb spick prick gets himself locked up right before Christmas. What kind of man, what kind of father ... I'm not gonna let him spoil the holidays for these kids, I'm not.

I'm sorry, Des, I didn't know. Was it ... did he get caught ... was it the tags?

Yea it was the tags. Him and his stupidass cousin. They're holding the two of them cuz his cousin's got a record, and Rico's got like five unpaid tickets. Rico said they'll be out before Christmas, he promises, but who knows Sal, who knows.

I'm sorry, I said again, and this time Desiree took my sorry and used it as a springboard for a tirade: Yea I'm sorry too. Sorry these kids might not have their father around for Christmas cuz he's still fucking around. We've been together since we were kids, Sal, kids, I was fourteen, he was fifteen, and he's still doing the same shit he did then. I tell him—you're a grown man now Rico, you gotta stop with this shit—and he tells me—(Desiree made her voice deep and Rico-like)—No but D. I've never been caught, you're worrying for nothing—(back to her regular voice)—Yea right Sal, I'm worrying for nothing. That's why he's in jail for the holidays and I'm here alone with the kids. That's his idea of nothing Sal.

Desiree vented for several more minutes and by time I got off the phone with her I was fully restored to a concrete reality that had no time for ghosts, time travel and word-spells. Desiree's gripes continued to echo in my head, but that quickly gave way to how Rico's incarceration would impact my life.

I poured myself another glass of club soda, then spread some peanut butter on Saltines and slowly crunched away on them as I realized that my only source of income was gone, at least for the foreseeable future. The inability to pay rent, pay bills, buy groceries, these things were the ordinary struggles of an ordinary man trapped in a traditional blues song—that I could handle—but if I couldn't afford to bring ghosting back into my life....

Stay calm, Sal, stay calm, I told myself, but anxiety like pins and needles began its malignant takeover. I was quick to employ my usual remedies—the repeated sharpening of pencils, the recitation of album titles, a scalding-hot shower—yet none of these worked and I was left paralyzed by a sense of gloom and doom. I curled up in the corner, near my sink, thinking dark useless thoughts. Keaton stared at me as if I were foreign matter then recognition clicked in his witch-doctor eyes and he sidled up alongside me.

Keaton, I said in a low voice, what's wrong with me?

Keaton didn't answer, didn't even raise his head to acknowledge that I had spoken to him, and I suddenly wanted to fling him across the room. Instead I beat my fists against my forehead until my hands ached and my head began to throb. My body began to weigh. I grew intensely sleepy and lay my head on the floor next to Keaton's. His breathing was steady and even, something I could count on, and this reminded me of my ghost, Y., which reminded me of Scandinavia. Scandinavia, I thought. I had forgotten about Scandinavia.

I pulled myself from the floor, as if being grabbed by the back of the neck, and went the few steps to my desk. I picked up a pencil, opened my notebook to a blank page and wrote the word Scandinavia. Nothing. I went back and re-read the random facts about Scandinavia. Nothing. No feeling whatsoever. The peephole was closed.

Somewhere outside of me Y. was in the cold, wanting a warm place to call home. Somewhere inside me I too was in the cold, wanting a warm place to call home.

II

When I woke the next day things didn't feel as dramatic. I was still slightly hungover from my ghosting, but it now felt like something that three cups of coffee and a dozen sharpened pencils could cure.

Re-establish ordinary rituals, I told myself, and you'll be fine. With the scripted efficiency of an automaton I went about my routine. I brewed coffee. Scrambled eggs. Fed Keaton. Borrowed my neighbor's Daily News. Read the backpage sports headline—Ole! Knicks Tame Bulls For Fourth Straight. Flipped to the boxscore and mentally penciled in all the action.

Things started to feel right inside, regular, and I imagined a new headline—Knicks Save Brooklyn Man From Himself. Story on pp. ____.

I hadn't been out of my apartment all week. I went to the window, which opened to a view of the courtyard below, and in the distance provided a generous view of the Verrazano Bridge. I opened it. A surge of cold air hit me in the face. It felt good and instantly roused my senses. I stared out at the Verrazano, its cables like strings on an instrument, shrouded in a pewter mist. Then I looked down and saw a boy and a girl, who I took to be brother and sister, milling around in the courtyard. They were both dressed in winter coats, with hats, gloves and scarves. The brother, who was taller and older than his sister, was trying to scrape up enough snow to pack a snowball. Except for scant traces the snow had gone, yet the boy was diligent: he scooped a little from one spot, a little from another, and soon had a pretty decent-sized snowball, which he immediately hurled at his unsuspecting sister. The snowball exploded against her chest and she began screaming bloody murder as she ran away, followed by her brother.

I pulled my head in from outside and closed the window. My earlobes, cheeks and the tip of my nose tingled.

Nine days until Christmas, I thought. I could see what Tania was doing for Christmas Eve and Christmas Day. Or I could drop in at Aunt Rosalie and Uncle Carmine's place. When my mother had died several years earlier from ovarian cancer, her sister, my Aunt Rosalie, had said to me—You're my son now. You come here for holidays, okay? You come here whenever you want. We want to see you, okay?

Since my mother's passing I had only gone to Rosalie's three or four times. She was a nice enough lady, and my Uncle Carmine was a sweetheart, but I had never felt a particularly strong connection with anyone in my family— except for my mother's mother, my Nona, Angie, who would read me stories—so my mother's death also meant the collapse of a bridge between myself and my relatives.

My father was a ghost—living or dead I had no idea—but I never knew him, not even his name, as my mother had only referred to him as The Bastard.

The Bastard knocked me up and left ... You wanna know where The Bastard is, he's in hell, that's where he is ... The Bastard is not your father, he's a piece-a-shit sperm donor.

Once, when I had asked my mother to tell me what The Bastard's real name was, she slapped me hard and said—The Bastard doesn't have a name . Do you understand?

I understood the force of the slap and never asked again.

There was a photo I had found in one of my mother's trunks, and while I can't say for certain, I'm pretty sure it's The Bastard with my mother in the photo. The photo is black-and-white and its borders are beige and scalloped. In the photo my mother and The Bastard are at the beach. My mother is seated on a striped beach towel, her legs tucked beneath her, her hands resting on her thighs. Her skin is dark, her hair cut in a bob, and she's a prototype of voluptuousness in her one-piece bikini. Her eyes are hidden behind dark oversized sunglasses. She reminds me of a fuller-figured and more ethnic version of Jackie O. The Bastard is next to her, balancing on one knee, his other leg arched at a right angle, and his hand is laid on my mother's shoulder. He's wearing swim trunks. There's not much to his chest and shoulders, and a small animal of a moustache that says porno star or detective darkly underlines his pronounced nose. His hair is longish and registers the same type of thick curls that my hair does. Both he and my mother are smiling, and in the background you can see several umbrellas staked in the sand, and beyond that the ocean.

After my mother died I had expected to find at least small traces of evidence that linked her to The Bastard and proved that they had had a relationship. Yet there had been nothing. Except me. And the photo. With an image that may or may not have reflected The Bastard.

After my third cup of coffee I called Tania at work.

Glad to know you still exist, she said. I haven't heard from you in almost two weeks.

I apologized for my negligence and told her I'd make it up to her by letting her take me out for dinner. Or drinks. Or both. Her choice.

You are shamelessly shameless, Tania laughed.

It wasn't truly true but I found it nice that Tania thought so.

What happened to your new career as a criminal, she asked. I thought you'd be making Boo Koo bucks?

Operations have been temporarily suspended, I said.

Tania laughed again—The best laid plans, huh? Ahrite, Sal, I'll call you during my lunch break and we'll come up with a plan for this evening. Okay?

Okay, I said, and hung up.

Maybe it was because it was the holidays, or maybe it was something that ghosting had triggered in me, but I found myself feeling strong feelings for Tania. Like when we were teenagers. I was in need of Tania's company and her attention, and for the first time in a long time I allowed my mind to contemplate a future with her. Tania was smart and beautiful and funny and kind. Why wouldn't I want her as my other? Or maybe the bigger question was—Why would she want me as her other?

I called Desiree to see if anything had changed in Rico's situation. It hadn't. Both he and his cousin were being held until they could see the judge, which wouldn't happen for at least another three days. Desiree's tone was no longer angry but weary and exasperated. She had to be at work at noon—she was a receptionist at a doctor's office—and her mother couldn't watch the kids because she had to work too.

I'm up to here in it, Desiree cracked, and I imagined her hand being held near or above the top of her head.

The words flew out of my mouth without forethought—I can watch the kids, Desi.

There was a pause followed by a high-pitched—Really? Oh Sal that would be HUGE. I get out of work at five and G.G. usually takes a nap around one or two. Sal you'd be a lifesaver.

Then I'm a lifesaver, I said. I'm just gonna shower and get dressed and I'll hop on the train.

About an hour later I arrived at Desiree and Rico's place, which was in Bensonhurst.

Look who's here, it's Uncle Sal, Desiree said as she braced against the wall while slipping on one of her heels. Victor held up a yellow dumptruck and said—Look what I got Uncle Sal.

His kid sister, Gina, who everyone called G.G., snatched the dump-truck from his hand, held it up and said—Look wha I gah Unca Sah.

Nooooo, Victor wailed, and a brief dumptruck-tug-of-war ensued, with Victor winning and G.G. spilled on the floor, crying.

Victor, Desiree snapped, as she scooped up the blubbering G.G. You don't make your sister fall and cry, you hear me, Desiree scolded.

But Ma she took my truck, Victor defended himself.

Desiree paid him no mind as she cradled G.G. and spoke to her in a soft voice—Mommy's gotta go to work now, sweepea. You're gonna stay with Uncle Sal, okay?

Noooo, G.G. screamed, and swelled her lips into a pout.

G.G. I'll be back soon, Desiree said. Give Mommy kisses.

No, G.G. said again, making her pout even poutier.

Yes, Desiree said and began tickling G.G. who squealed like an animatronic doll. When Desiree was done tickling G.G., she said—Give Mommy kisses. G.G. complied and planted several wet kisses on and around Desiree's mouth.

Did you smudge Mommy's lipstick, Desiree asked. G.G. nodded enthusiastically. Desiree handed G.G. to me, then kneeled down until she was eye-level with Victor and said— You're gonna be a good boy for Uncle Sal, right?

Victor lowered his eyes and nodded.

That's my big dad, Desiree said as she embraced Victor and kissed him on the mouth. Desiree rose to standing and rapidly explained to me where the essentials were, what needed to happen, and if I needed to call—number's on the fridge.

Thanks a million Sal, Desiree said, pecked me on the cheek, and rushed off.

I sat down on the couch, G.G. grafted to my hip.

Cartoons, she said, and pointed at the TV, its glaring screen about fifty inches, playing in surround-sound. Tom & Jerry was on and Tom was about to deliver a crushing mallet-blow to Jerry. SLAM. Tom missed Jerry and instead whacked his foot, which swelled, turned pink and began beating like a heart. G.G. laughed and pointed at the screen.

Cat, she said.

Yea cat, I confirmed.

Victor had immersed himself in the hodgepodge of toys that littered the living-room floor—mostly cars, trucks and action figures. It was his own slice-of-paradise and he was happily lost there, completely oblivious to mine and his sister's existence.

While Victor played, G.G. and I fell into a Tom-and-Jerry trance. When the show was over I went into the kitchen, G.G. in tow, and microwaved the chicken nuggets that Desiree had told me to feed the kids for lunch. When the nuggets were done I took out two containers of Mott's applesauce, which I set on the plate next to the nuggets.

By time G.G. finished eating her entire face was painted in applesauce. She smiled at me as if she were aware and proud of her artistic makeover. G.G. had her mother's dark hair and blue eyes. Her hair was bound in two fountain-spray pigtails. Victor, like Rico, had a buzz-cut, and his eyes were large, warm and brown.

Shortly after lunch G.G. conked out and I placed her in her crib. Victor returned to his paradise. I sat down on the couch to read a hip-hop magazine that I had found in the kitchen. Biggie was on the cover with a vicious scowl on his face and his middle-finger thrust forward. I clicked off the TV and even though Victor hadn't been watching it, he wailed—No-no-no. Don't shut it off. Don't shut it.

Why, I asked.

You gotta leave it on, it's gotta stay on, Victor said, distress widening his eyes. I clicked it back on—The Flintstones—and Barney Rubble's goofy laugh filled the room. Victor didn't look at the screen but he instantly relaxed. About a minute later he abandoned his toys and joined me on the couch.

Hello, he said, and stared at me, smiling.

Hello Victor, I said, and put down the magazine. What's up?

Victor shrugged and kept staring. His stare felt like the innocent and vulnerable sibling to Anna's stare. Where her intense gaze had made me feel ashamed of the fact that I existed, his made me feel aware of myself as a human who might be of some use. What do you need Victor, I thought but didn't say. Our eyes remained locked and I waited for Victor to speak, expecting something profound or philosophical to come out of his mouth.

You're a buttman, Victor said and giggled, covering his mouth with his hands. Then he began squeal-repeating—Buttman, buttman, buttman—and eventually his laughter broke up into hiccups.

Here, I said, and handed him a bottle of Poland Spring. He glugged and when he was done

he handed me the bottle and went right back to buttmanning, phrasing it in different ways:

Sal is a buttman (sing-song) ... You're a buttman, you're a buttman (a cheer) ... ButtmanButtmanButtman (speed metal) ... Are you a buttman, yes I am (Q &A).

It took almost five minutes before Victor got tired of buttmania.

What do you want to do now, I asked him. Should we read a book?

Yeaaaa, Victor screamed, and I pressed my finger against my lips—Sssshhh, you'll wake up G.G. Which I then realized was ridiculous since you couldn't hear a shotgun blast over the volume of the TV.

Victor ran to his bedroom and came back with A Christmas Carol. It was a picture-book version meant for young children. Victor crawled into my lap and I could feel him bristling with excitement.

Do you know Scrooge, he asked me.

Yea I know Scrooge.

He was bad then he was good. The ghosts helped him to be good.

Yes the ghosts helped him, I agreed, and was about to start reading but Victor kept on—They were good ghosts, right Uncle Sal?

Yea they were good ghosts. They were useful.

Use-ful, Victor said, as if trying the word on for size. Then—But there are bad ghosts too, right? Ghosts that want to take you away. But they won't take me, right?

No Victor they won't take you, I assured him. You're safe.

And G.G. too?

G.G.'s safe too.

And you. You safe Uncle Sal?

I'm safe Victor. We're all safe.

Victor smiled and buried his head in my chest,

corkscrewing his skull into my pectoral. When he was done he sat up straight and said—Okay read.

Except for the scary uprising that took place in G.G.'s diaper, the rest of the afternoon went smoothly. Desiree got home a little before 5:30 and was lovingly attacked by her kids. She handed me a brown bag and said—Look what one of my bosses gave me as a Christmas gift.

I slid a bottle out of the bag: Polly-Fuisse.

Looks like good shit, huh, Desiree said.

Good shit indeed, I said and placed the bottle in the fridge.

Desiree dispatched Victor to the living room to clean up his toys, and placed G.G. in her high-chair, which she then turned toward the thirteen-inch TV that was set on the counter. Desiree flipped channels until Barney appeared. G.G. gave him a rousing ovation. Desiree went to the kitchen window and cracked it open. Then she sat on the sill and lit a cigarette.

How was it, she asked.

Fine just fine.

Ready for one of your own?

Not at all.

It's not easy.

No I can't imagine it is.

Wouldn't ask for refunds though. Once they're here they're here. And you love em like crazy.

I nodded and smiled. Desiree leaned down, blew smoke out the window, then said—I got some beef empanadas left over from last night. I can heat those up, nuke some creamed spinach ... stay and have dinner with us. We can drink that fancy wine.

I accepted Desiree's offer then remembered about Tania.

Can I use your phone, Des, I asked.

Yea-yea.

I called Tania's job and was told that I had just missed her. Then I called her house and left a message on her machine, explaining my impromptu babysitting gig. I'll try you again in a little while, I said, and hung up.

Desiree, who was loading a tray of empanadas into the oven, said—Tania, that's the tall Russian girl, right?

Yea.

Didn't you two used to go out?

Yea. Way back when.

What happened?

Nothing. We're just better as friends.

Yea, Desiree said, you wouldn't wanna end up like me and Rico ... married enemies.

Desiree's head was turned so I couldn't see if she was smiling or not. She took a package of creamed spinach out of the freezer, placed it in a bowl, then into the microwave. Then she turned to me—You know me and Rico been together fourteen years?

That's a long time, I said.

Tell me about it. But the way I see it—Rico might be a dumb spick but he's my dumb spick. And he's got a real good heart, y'know?

I know, I said, and flashed back to the time when Rico and I were at a Sweet Sixteen, and a kid named Mikey G. was also there with several of his boys. They wanted to jump me because I had made out with Mikey's ex-girlfriend, Lisa. When I left the party they were all waiting outside for me and Mikey got in my face and said—You messed around with my girl Lisa. I said nothing and just stared into Mikey G's narrowed eyes, looking for an angle.

Next thing I know Rico rushed outside and came between me and Mikey, chest-nudging Mikey back several inches.

You got beef with my boy, Rico spoke into Mikey's face, to which Mikey responded—I ain't got beef with you Rico.

That's when Rico took out a knife, held it against Mikey's cheek and repeated—You got beef with my boy?

Mikey didn't say anything and his friends didn't move a muscle. Then Rico sniffed the inside of Mikey's neck and said—Thought I smelled a pussy. You and your faggotass friends get the fuck outta here.

Strength in numbers lost to neighborhood reputation as Mikey G. and his boys beat a hasty retreat.

The microwave beeped three short beeps. Out came the creamed spinach. Victor came into the kitchen, gave a passing glance to the prancing purple dinosaur on TV, then said—Mommy I cleaned up.

Very good, dad, Desiree said as she spooned the creamed spinach into a bowl.

Mommy Uncle Sal is a buttman, Victor said, craning his neck up to his mother.

Is he, Desiree said, and looked at me, smiling.

What can I say the kid's got me pegged.

Victor launched into a buttman chant which Desiree quickly cut off—That's enough dad. Sit down, we're gonna eat.

Victor quietly obeyed. Then: Mommy where's daddy?

Fuck me, Desiree yelped, as she burned her finger while taking the tray out of the oven. She quickly began sucking on it then ran it under cold water.

You okay Mommy, Victor checked.

Yea I'm fine, she said, and turned off the water.

Following the lead of the purple dinosaur, G.G. broke into song—I love you, you love me, we're a happy family ... with a great big hug and a kiss from me to you, won't you say you love me too?

When the song was done G.G. blew kisses at Barney, who waved back at her and the billion other kids who kept him in business.

Okay time to eat, Desiree said. Sal can you get the wine.

We ate dinner, Desiree eating in fits and starts as she had to negotiate both G.G. and Victor's eating. After dinner I washed dishes while Desiree gave the kids a bath. Once they were clean she set them up in the living room with a movie: The Jungle Book.

Desiree and I sat in the kitchen, drinking wine, Desiree smoking out the window. At one point she got up, took a pill bottle out the cabinet, and tapped a pink pill into her hand. You want a Perc, she asked me.

No I'm good, I said then quickly switched tracks—Yea I'll have one.

We washed down our Percs with Polly-Fuisse and our talk quickly turned to Christmas.

We're gonna put up the tree tomorrow. I was gonna wait for Rico but ... I'm not gonna wait.

He'll be out before Christmas, I said with prophetic certainty.

Yea probably, Desiree said flatly. What are you doing for Christmas?

I don't know yet.

You're welcome to come over here on Christmas Eve. My mom will be here and probably some of Rico's family. My mom's gonna make roasted chicken.

Thanks, maybe I'll drop by.

A short silence followed as Desiree puffed away on her cigarette. I refilled our wine glasses then asked Desiree what she thought about ghosts.

Ghosts, she said and laughed. Why you asking me that?

Just curious what you think, I said.

Desiree took a meditative pull on her cigarette then answered—I don't know. I kinda don't believe in them but at the same time the idea of them freaks me out. So I don't know. You being haunted Sal, Desiree said and smiled.

We are haunted. Wait for the epilogue. That phrase flashed in my mind. What was it from? Where had I read or heard it?

No I'm not haunted, I said. I just ... ghosts fascinate me.

Well here's to the Ghost of Christmas Future, Desiree said and raised her glass.

I did the same and repeated—To the Ghost of Christmas Future.

We clinked glasses.

I left Desiree's at about eight, with Victor crying for me

to stay. Even though the temperature was in the teens I decided to walk home. I had my walkman and listened to a mixed tape I had made. Miles Davis, Tom Waits, Nina Simone, Bjork and Public Enemy kept me company as I strolled along at a leisurely pace.

When I got to 12th Avenue and 84th Street there were droves of people who had come out to see the Dyker Lights. Every year, during the holidays, three avenues—11th to 13th— on three different streets—83rd to 86th, were turned into a festive wonderland, with houses decked out in their holiday best. There was competitiveness to the displays as you could tell that every house wanted to outdo the others in terms of size or uniqueness.

I made my way through the crowd and drank in the various sights. Wooden toy soldiers that stood about ten feet high, standing guard in an entranceway to a stately home. Another house whose front lawn doubled as a ballet stage, with mechanized ballerinas pirouetting to The Nutcracker Suite. Then there was an inflatable Santa, who looked to be twenty-five to thirty-feet high, crowding the front porch of a house, which was flanked by illuminated angel sculptures. On the curbside I encountered Frosty the Snowman, who was offering free mull wine to passer-bys. He ladled some into a plastic cup for me and wished me a happy yuletide. I drank the wine which was warming and deliciously tart.

As I continued my walk home I had a good feeling in the pit of my stomach, or perhaps it was somewhere deeper in my being, and decided to call Tania from a payphone.

Hello, came Tania's voice.

Hey T., you got my message?

Yea-yea. I just got home. I went out for drinks after work with some of my co-workers.

The thickness in Tania's voice told me that she was drunk, or at least buzzed.

Feeling good, I asked her.

Yeaaa. And you?

Best of spirits.

You home?

No I'm calling from a payphone. I'm on my way home.

You babysat?

Yea. I watched Desiree and Rico's kids.

Maybe you found your calling, Tania said, then I heard a male voice in the background ask—Bathroom?

That one, Tania said to the male voice, then to me—Sal?

Yea I'm here. I swallowed. Who's there?

Oh that's someone I work with, my friend Teddy.

Ahrite I'll let you go then, I said.

Do you want to meet up tomorrow, Tania asked. I'm not working.

Yea maybe, I said, I'll call you tomorrow.

Okay, Mr. Sal, stay in good spirits.

I hung up the phone, Tania's words continuing to echo in my head. My friend Teddy ... My friend Teddy ... My friend Teddy.

The good feeling in the pit of my stomach had been displaced by sharp pangs of jealousy. What the fuck is your problem Sal, I said to myself. Tania's not your girlfriend and even if she were she was hanging out with her friend Teddy. Her friend. Teddy is a friend. Tania had a friend whose name was Teddy. Friend Teddy. Friend.

My mind kept on in this way for a while, prompting me to play my music at peak-volume in an attempt to drown out the Teddy sessions. I drew strength from Chuck D.'s baritone rap-attack, as he bulldozed his way through "Bring the Noise." Friend Teddy couldn't stand up to that, and to keep myself feeling streetcorner and concrete I did something I hadn't done since I was a teenager: I stopped at a bodega and bought a 40 oz. of St. Ides.

When I got home I drank about half of it before I called Tania again. Her machine came on and I left a message in a stranger's voice: We are haunted. Wait for the epilogue.

After I hung up I noticed Keaton staring at me with accusation in his eyes.

What, I said, challenging Keaton with my voice.

He yawned and padded away. Shortly after that I passed
out.

III

Sunday I woke up late, feeling groggy and out of sorts. Tania called in the afternoon but I didn't pick up.

Was that you who left that weird message on my machine last night, came Tania's voice over my machine.

If you want to hang out later, give me a call.

My plan was to spend the rest of day in the company of two silent clowns. I was going to drink lots of tea, embed myself in my futon, and marathon-view all the Chaplin and Keaton films that I owned.

Afternoon became evening and evening dissolved into night. I was happily immersed in a world of flickering black and white. I dozed off in the middle of Sherlock, Jr., and had another dream about Laura Ciccerone. This time she was one of the mechanized ballerinas dancing to The Nutcracker Suite. Laura is that you, I shouted at her several times, but she didn't respond, just kept pirouetting, as the image of her and the other ballerinas went in and out of focus. I awoke with a start, and a dry mouth.

I drank two glasses of water then ejected Sherlock, Jr. from my VCR and slid in a tape that was a compilation of Keaton shorts. Buster, stone-faced and nimble-footed, was navigating through a series of pratfalls when the phone rang. I looked at the clock. 11:26. I ignored the ringing and soon a flinty voice came over my machine.

Heya is this Sal Sal this is Henry I'm a friend of Jimmy's Told me to give you a call So I'm calling you home?

While I hadn't forgotten about Jimmy, his existence had become more and more unreal and remote with each passing day. Yet hearing his name spoken aloud by this stranger's voice gave me a jolt of recognition. Jimmy Barrone: the writer, the kid you grew up with, the disappeared.

I picked up. Hello this is Sal.

Hey Sal heya. The fuzziness in the man's voice, and the patter in the background, indicated to me that he was calling from a bar.

The man, Henry, went on to explain how he and Jimmy had hung out the other night—they were drinking buddies—and Jimmy had told him he was leaving for North Carolina and had no idea when he'd be back. As a send-off he and Jimmy had drunk themselves sideways, and before Jimmy left he gave Henry my phone number and said—Make sure you call my buddy Sal. He's someone who gets it. Tell him about North Carolina and tell him that Jimmy said stay curious.

Why hadn't Jimmy called me directly, I wondered. And North Carolina ... something to do with Laura Ciccerone?

Henry and I decided to meet at The Diving Mermaid the next day. It's this bar on Neptune & 16th where me and Jimmy drink, he'd said in peculiar, unpunctuated phrasings. let's say four   happy hour starts at four   it'll be easy to find me   look for the dwarf.

And that was that. I was to meet Henry the dwarf at four at the Diving Mermaid on Neptune & 16th.

I felt a sudden revival of blood-passion inside me. I was back on the case. Yet was there even a case to be back on? Henry had seen and hung out with Jimmy and hadn't reported anything strange about his behavior, except for the fact that Jimmy had gone to North Carolina. Which, whether motivated by Laura Ciccerone or not, wasn't all that strange. Still, there was the business about fractals and being dead and until I got some clear-cut answers from Jimmy himself, or some other viable source ... the case wasn't closed.

On Monday I heard from Rico, who had gotten out. He told me that he was taking a temporary vacation from tag-switching, and reiterated Desiree's invitation for me to spend Christmas Eve at their place.

I left at 3 o' clock and took the R train to Stillwell. There was an ice-prickly wind rolling in off the Atlantic and I hastily made my way to Neptune & 16th. The Diving Mermaid was located just off the corner. A wooden mermaid in need of a makeover was posted above the entrance. I walked through the front door and the instant shift from bright cold to warm dark was comforting.

The crowd was sparse and the place modest-sized. The interior was an L-shape in reverse, with a half-dozen tables occupying the inside of the L. The bar ran parallel to the tables, about twenty feet of floor-space between them. A Battlestar Galactica pinball machine and an old-fashioned jukebox dominated the background. The TV that was mounted in a corner, at the far end of the bar, was tuned to ESPN. At the end of the bar, closest to the front door, I saw a dwarf drinking a mug of dark beer. I went over and said his name.

Henry whip-snapped his head and when he saw me shouted—Heya pal—as if I were a dear old friend of his that he was overjoyed to see.

Good to know ya Sal good to know ya, Henry said, and pumped my hand vigorously.

You wanna sit here or at a table let's go sit at a table heya Frank I'm gonna move to a table.

What I had first heard on the phone was even more pronounced in person. Henry spoke in jittery staccato bursts and jabs that challenged my equilibrium. His breath between word-flurries was a quick hard sucking of air, just enough oxygen to keep going.

Henry slid off his stool, mug in hand, and with a noticeable limp led me to a table near the jukebox.

Henry couldn't have been more than four feet tall. He was wearing a pea-green overcoat, which fit him big, and a coal-grey cap. The overcoat was badly frayed and its buttons dangled precariously. Fire-orange hair, with a greasy sheen, spilled out the sides and back of his cap and cut off just above his shoulders. A natty fire-orange beard covered his face, which was a geological masterpiece of crags, grooves and contours. His nose, a chewed-up pink marshmallow, protruded from the center of it.

The bartender Frank came over. He was a solid-looking

man with neatly combed white hair and cloud-fluff for eyebrows. He placed a cocktail napkin in front of me and said—What are you drinking?

What are you drinking, I asked Henry.

I was drinking Murphy's, Henry responded after draining the rest of what had been in his mug. I'll have another, he said to Frank, and a shot of Wild Turkey.

I'll do a Murphy's minus the Wild Turkey, I said to Frank.

Right, Frank said and left.

Henry was about to say something to me then exploded into a dry hacking cough. He placed his pudgy hand over his mouth and continued coughing as his body violently shook and tears came into his eyes. When the fit finally ended Henry took his hand away from his mouth and stared at his palm. Then he looked at me and wheezed—Half a lung and then some. He cackled and wiped his hand on his coat.

Frank returned with our drinks. You want to pay as you go or run a tab, he asked me.

Henry cut in: Anything he drinks Frank goes on my tab put em on my tab.

Will do, Hen, Frank said and left.

Henry quickly shot back his Wild Turkey and slammed the empty glass down on the table. Then he said: Call me Hen Sal all my friends call me Hen know why they call me Hen?

I ventured a guess. It's short for Henry.

Henry rattled a chest-deep laugh. Yea-yea that's part of it Hen's short for Henry but there's another reason my cock I have a great cock a big one and I like to use it don't worry only on women so you see Sal I'm Hen the cock.

I don't get it, I said. The hen's the female, the rooster's the cock.

Hen laughed again. Yea-yea I know but we already got a rooster Freddy the Red Rooster he's not here now but he's a regular don't know why they call him the Red Rooster not cuz of his cock I don't think plus like you said Hen's short for Henry Rooster's not short for anything.

Hen unbuttoned his overcoat and pointed at his chest.

See this, he said, see the T-shirt I'm wearing.

Hen held his coat open as I read the words printed on his T-shirt:

No Man Is An Island
But Women Sure Are Beaches!

The words were accompanied by a peeling decal image of a man—a hard-on tenting his shorts—ogling a woman in a bikini, who was lying in the sand.

Only three things I give a shit about Sal, Henry said. He put up one finger—Pussy—then another—Booze—and a third—Art. Those are the three things that keep me going.

Hen said it again, this time compounding the three words into one: PussyBoozeArt.

It sounded like a fancy French wine. Or swinging nightclub.

Hen went on to explain how he was a painter and that he and Jimmy had often closed down the Mermaid rambling about art and literature.

You wanna see something amazing, Hen said, then rose to his feet and toddled unevenly over to the bar. I followed.

Look at that, he said, and pointed at a framed piece of parchment paper that hung on the wall behind the bar. In elegant stylized print that looked like it could have been written with a fountain pen, it read:

What things have we seen
Done at the Mermaid!
Heard words that have been so nimble, and full of subtle flame,
As if that every one from whence they came
Had meant to put his whole life within a jest,
And had resolved to live a fool the rest of his dull life.
—Francis Beaumont to Ben Jonson

That's amazing don't you think, Hen said. When you

think about it a bar in Coney Island a bar that's not a mansy-pansy poet-bar has got this beautymark on the wall   That's Frank for you   The Mermaid's his place y'know   guy really knows his stuff   sports science art film   guy reads everything a real Renaissance guy   and his bar's named after the stuff of romantic poets   well that and Coney Island's got mermaid history lot of mermaid history here.

I took in what Hen said then looked over at Frank, who was drawing beer from a tap. I surveyed the rest of what Frank's walls had to offer. Photos of baseball players, boxers, entertainers. Archival prints of Coney Island. An isolated photo of a bearded Hemingway and a dark-skinned man holding up what looked like a marlin.

I could see why Jimmy would love this place. If he had dreamed up his ideal spot to drink and gab and carouse, the end-result would've looked and felt a lot like the Mermaid.

Hen and I ordered another round and went back to our table. I asked him if he had seen Jimmy a lot in the past month.

Just that one time two days ago I said where you been Jimmy and he said here and there that's what he said here and there.

Did he seem different when you saw him, I asked Hen.

Different like how.

I don't know. Troubled. Or not his usual self.

Troubled is Jimmy's usual self, Hen cracked. Jimmy's Jimmy.

I spent the next fifteen minutes spilling the beans about Jimmy's phone call, and everything that had come after. Ghosting, the tape recorder, Laura Ciccerone, Anna.

Do you know Anna, I asked Hen.

No but by your description I'd like to   I'd like to know Anna from the inside-in know what I mean.

I asked Hen what Jimmy had been up to in the past several months.

Up to like how.

Was he working?

You know Jimmy   he takes whatever shit gig he can to stay afloat   think his last gig   he was a moving man   Jimmy hates work   less it's writing   I'm the same   except for me it's painting   I've got a fixed income though   so.

Several hours passed and the Mermaid filled up. The air grew thick with cigarette smoke and dialogue. Hen had drunk about double the amount that I had. His eyes had a syrupy glaze and froth had migrated from the corners of his mouth to his beard. The jukebox was playing The Eagles "Desperado." The man who had picked the song stood next to the jukebox and lip-synced with his eyes closed. He also made dramatic gestures that seemed a sign language for the dispossessed. Or the heartbroken.

The comforting bar-dark of the Mermaid had worked its way deep inside me and I didn't want to leave. I felt like Jimmy's understudy, as Hen and I talked about sports and art and literature. Then there was the history and folklore of Coney Island, of which Hen was an aficionado. As he talked and talked and in serrated chickenscratch, I scrawled down random facts on numerous cocktail napkins.

    Coney Island formerly an island
    now a peninsula w/ landfill
    connecting it to Brooklyn

    The Lenape (indians) who inhabited
    the island called it—Narrioch—land without shadows
    cuz its position keeps the beach
    in sunlight all day

    Coney Island from the Dutch—Conyne Eylandt—
    Rabbit Island
    cuz of the diverse rabbit population before
    resort development destroyed their habitat.

    1885 to 1886—the Coney Island Elephant
    A hotel & brothel

The first sight to greet immigrants arriving in NYC
(not Statue of Liberty)

The night wore on. And the steady increase in females at
the Mermaid brought out a predatory Hen. He openly leered
at women, made shameless passes, and occasionally barked
or howled at them. One woman, who didn't take too kindly to
Hen's placement of his hand, yanked his beard, called him a
dirty little midget, and stormed off.

Hen looked at me with liquid fire in his eyes and said—
Stupid cow   I don't mind being insulted but at least do it
accurately   I'm a dwarf not a midget   a midget's body is small
but rightly proportioned   do I look rightly proportioned to
you   and you haven't even seen my cock.

Hen paused, took a sip of the port wine he had switched
to, and concluded—Know what Voltaire said   God's a
comedian playing to an audience too afraid to laugh   I'm not
afraid to laugh   ugly dwarf body big beautiful cock   trust me I
laugh.

Eventually Hen got lucky when Josie, a large woman with
a bright pink face and clinking bracelets, joined us. She was a
regular who Hen knew well and he ordered her a White
Russian. Then another. And another.

When Josie went to use the bathroom Hen took my hand
and gave it an emphatic squeeze.

Our time's up for tonight pal   I'm gonna take Josie home
and give her the Hen special   gotta stay on top though
otherwise Fat Lady Smotherfucks Dwarf to Death news at 11
know what I mean.

Anyway let's hang out again   you're a bit of alright   like
the Brits say   next time come to my place and I'll show you my
paintings see what ya think   if you wanna stick around and
keep drinking fine just put em on my tab   the Mermaid's a bit
of alright ain't it.

I agreed that it was and told Hen I'd call him soon. Josie
came back from the bathroom and when she saw Hen
standing she asked him where he was going, to which he

responded—Home. With you hotsy-totsy.

Josie laughed and waved her hands as if not taking Hen seriously. Five minutes later they left together.

I went over to the bar, which was shoulder-to-shoulder packed with people watching Monday Night Football. Giants vs. Eagles. I ordered another pint of Murphy's and watched the game until halftime. Then I wished Frank a merry Christmas and left.

Outside the icy winds blowing in off the ocean had grown even fiercer, yet the alcohol in my system immunized me against the cold. I stood on the curb and stared up at the time-scarred mermaid. The red of her hair and the blue of her fish-body had flaked and peeled. I tried to recall the poem on the parchment paper but couldn't.

I started walking to the train station and when I was almost there I changed my mind. I went to Nathan's and bought two hot dogs, loaded with sauerkraut, relish, mustard and ketchup, and wolfed them down. I decided to go to the boardwalk.

It had to be around ten and the boardwalk was mostly empty. I stood at the railing and looked out at the beach, then past the beach to the ocean. Undulating tar or oil that brightened with ribbons of foam when the waves broke. The night-sky, which was a lighter shade of dark than the ocean, was well-endowed with stars. White, shimmering, cursive. In comparison the moon was a faded smudge, a spectral thumbprint.

Beautiful isn't it, came a voice so close its breath tickled my ear.

I turned and practically rubbed noses with the woman to whom the voice belonged. Anna.

Anna, I said, her name a catch in my throat. Whatever words were going to follow were blocked by that name, which I dumbly repeated—Anna.

Sal, Anna said, then again, Sal—as if delivering two kisses, one on each cheek. Anna was dressed in a puffy red parka and matching ski hat. The dark of Anna's hair and the white of her skin perfectly mirrored the dark of the ocean and the white of the stars. Anna braced her elbows on the railing and leaned forward.

I love the sea at night, she said, and stared out dreamily. I thought I could make out moisture in her eyes. Or maybe I was seeing her eyes through the moisture in my own. What with the cold and the alcohol.

Listen, Anna gently commanded. I listened.

The sound of gaseous fizz as the waves broke on the shoreline.

Champagne for a mermaid, Anna said, then turned to me, smiled and asked—Been drinking Salvo?

Yea, I confessed. I ... I went to meet someone who knows Jimmy. One of his drinking buddies. His name is Henry. Hen.

Anna nodded, returning her gaze to the sea. Then: Was this Henry Hen a nice man?

He's ... how would I put it? He's got a lot of vinegar in his soul. Pepper too.

Marvelous, Anna burst, as if I had just won something, and clapped her gloved hands together.

Anna, I started, then came the pause in which her name usually got stuck and sealed in anything else I might say. This time I pushed and the words kept coming—Anna, what is all this? What's going on?

What is what, Anna said with an innocence that sounded too sincere to be true.

This, I continued with urgency. All of this. The stuff with Jimmy, the things he said, and you ... who are you?

Sal, Anna spoke gently, Jimmy's your friend, right?

Yea.

You grew up together, didn't you?

Yea.

Friends develop bonds, Anna explained. Good friends develop strong bonds. Great friends develop even stronger bonds.

Yea, and?

And nothing Sal. Jimmy and you were friends. Bonds

were forged.

What do you mean were?

What do you mean what do you mean were?

I felt dizzy. Lou Costello on the tail-end of a schtick.

You said were and not are. Jimmy and I were friends. Not are friends.

A slip in tense, Anna said and smiled big. Her smile had a way of diverting me from the bits that dangled.

Neither one of us spoke for almost a minute. The alcohol had mostly worn off and I no longer felt immune to the cold.

Finally, Anna said—Do you want to go home?

No, I snapped, as if I were son to a mother who had just threatened him with punishment.

We can both go, Anna said softly.

To my place?

Yes.

I imagined me and Anna seated together on the R train, en route to my apartment. The notion seemed too fantastical and out-of-reach. Like kissing Madonna on the mouth. Or playing Jordan one-on-one.

Okay, I said, let's go back to my place.

Good, Anna said, then reached out and turned up the collar of my coat.

You've gotta stay warm, she said.

Yea, I nodded, my insides turning to mush.

Anna and I walked to the train station. I had hoped she would lock her arm inside mine as we walked but she kept her hands stuffed in her coat-pockets. Despite the fact that we had the walk to the train station, the ride on the train, and the walk from the train station to my apartment to talk to Anna, I spoke not a single word. Not because I didn't want to but because I had lost the power of speech. I was trapped in a silent film where nothing was black and white.

My apartment. Anna took off her coat and hat and gloves and handed them to me—Here—as if I were her servant. I was happy to do her bidding. As had happened with Claire, Keaton immediately bonded with Anna.

He rubbed against her leg and she picked him up, looked him square in the eye, and said—Hello, Ludwig.

His name's Keaton, I informed her, my voice having returned to me.

Really, she said, with great surprise. Are you a Keaton, Ludwig? Or are you a Ludwig, Keaton?

Keaton emitted a three-syllable meow. Anna tossed her head back and laughed. She cradled Keaton in her arms and rocked him like a baby. Then she sang him a peppy song in what sounded like German.

When she was done, I asked—What was that?

An old German lullaby. Schlef kindlen schlef.

You speak German?

Instead of answering my question directly, Anna said—It's a pastime of mine to know as many different lullabies in as many different languages as I can.

Do you know one in Swedish, I asked.

Without pause Anna broke into a new lullaby, this one slow and haunting.

When she finished she kept her eyes lowered. I felt hushed inside.

What was that one?

Byssan Lull.

What does Byssan Lull mean?

It doesn't mean anything. Byssan Lull is just Byssan Lull. The lullaby tells about preparing a kettle for three wanderers. The first has a limp, the second is blind, and the third doesn't say anything.

I nodded, the lullaby's sedative-effect continuing to linger.

I'm going to put water on for tea, I said. Would you like some?

No, Anna said, as she buried her nose in Keaton's fur and nuzzled him. I could feel his pleasure as if it were my own.

Anna came up for air and said—Do you have any orange soda?

No I don't.

I have a sudden hankering for orange soda, Anna said, then repeated—orange soda—with gleeful verve.

Can we get some, she asked.

Yea if you really want it.

I do. Orange soda would be mmmmmm.

Okay. There's a bagel store just around the corner. I can run over there—

Do you want me to come—

No, no, stay. Keaton's happy in your arms. I'll be back in five minutes.

Anna began singing another lullaby to Keaton, this one in French, as I left.

When I got back I didn't see Anna. My stomach froze then dropped.

Anna, I called out. No answer. Anna, orange soda delivery.

Yay, came the cheer as Anna emerged from the bathroom. My heart resumed its regular beating.

You have radiant heating in your floors, Anna said.

Yea, one of the perks of this place.

It's marvelous, she said, my toes are all toasty.

I looked down and saw Anna's toes wriggling in her socks.

I got you a six-pack of Fanta, I said. Do you want a glass?

No straight out of the can.

I snapped one from the plastic and handed it to her.

She popped the tab, guzzled, announced—Done—and burped ... in a fluid unbroken sequence. Then she burped again, this time covering her ears with her hands.

I got the fizzy tingles, she squealed.

Even though the woman who stood before me looked like a goddess, her present demeanor was that of a carbonated six-year-old.

Anna, my mother, now Anna, my daughter.

Give me another one, Anna said, and I handed her a can. I fixed myself a cup of Smoky Russian and we sat in the living room: I, on the recliner; Anna, on the futon.

Anna was happy to talk about the radiant heating in my

floors, about Keaton, about the virtues of orange soda, but when the subject was Jimmy, or herself, she was elusive and obscure.

How do you and Jimmy know each other?
Oh, me and Jimmy have a strange, deep and complicated relationship. In some ways it's a non-relationship.
When did you last see Jimmy?
I see Jimmy all the time. I've got eyes in the back of my eyes. And those eyes have eyes as well. This remark was followed by a gigglefit that made Anna sound like a doll on meth
What do you do for a living?
I breathe Sal. Isn't that what everyone does for a living?
Do you live in Brooklyn, the city? Somewhere else?
Did you know that Fanta, which comes from the German word "fanataise," which means "imagination," started in Germany in 1941?
Every question I asked Anna only led to more questions, which I didn't bother to ask. Our conversation continued in this roundabout way for a while, then: Do you slow-dance?
Slow-dance, I repeated.
Yes dancing that's not fast. Slow-dancing.
Yea, I know, I ... yea, I guess.
I see you have a record player. And records. Why don't you pick a song that we can slow-dance to? Or better yet— Anna sprang to her feet—I'll pick one.
Anna drained the rest of what had been her fourth Fanta, handed me the empty can, and walked over to the dresser upon which my record player and records were set. She breezily made her way through the stack of records, occasionally remarking—Oh they're great—or—She's tops.
Then she held up an album and said—This one.
It was Linda Ronstadt's Don't Cry Now.
We're going to slow-dance to Desperado, okay?
I nodded.
Anna removed the record from its sleeve and placed it on

the table. She lowered the needle—a prologue of scratchiness followed by piano.

Anna held out her arms and invited me into her space. I entered it, reluctantly, my stomach in knots.

Her long extraordinary fingers interlocked with my lesser, ordinary fingers. She placed her other hand on the small of my back. Linda Ronstadt pumped out pathos as Anna and I swayed. I felt as if the floor were moving and not my feet.

Anna laid her head in a cleft between my shoulder and neck. Her dark hair tumbled into my face. I breathed it in.

Nostalgia struck hard and something in me broke open.

Do you shampoo with Scandinavia, I asked in a weak voice.

Anna responded by singing along with Miss Ronstadt:

Oh freedom, well that's just some people talkin,
your prison is walking through this world all alone.

I seized up. The singing, the breath, the hair, Scandinavia, all of it became too much and I leaned in to kiss Anna. She quickly turned her head and my kiss landed awkwardly on her cheek.

What are you doing, she said.

I—was all I could manage—to which Anna responded— Yes, you—and began laughing. In my face. The laugh wasn't malicious or amused, it was something else altogether, something I couldn't classify.

Anna went to the record player and turned it off. She was still laughing. I felt prickly heat in my face and hands.

I didn't think it was that funny, I snapped.

Anna tried to snort-stop her laughter, which she eventually got under control.

Oh Salvo, it's not funny at all, she said. And yet it is. If only, then she paused and her expression became thoughtful.

Let me put it this way, she continued, if that kiss had gone any further, it if had become—how do they say—big with flames—no that's not it—hot and heavy, yes—and you were to have entered me, do you know what it would have been like?

What, I asked, curious and aroused.

Like—and Anna's voice shifted to a philosophical baritone, deep and a little bit scary: The angels are white burning white and the eye that insists on confronting them shrivels.

What does that mean, I said.

It means—and Anna repeated the phrase in the same ominous baritone.

Even though I still had no idea what she was talking about, something did register somewhere, and my mind fixated on the word "shrivel," relating it not to my eye but to my dick.

The notion of sex between me and Anna stridently flew out the window.

Anna stared at me with an incisive yet somehow merciful gaze. I grew small. Anna was my mother again.

Anna, I asked in a quiet voice, are you a ghost?

Anna smiled and said—What's my name?

Anna. If that is your name.

Anna, she repeated, as if confirming it. Not X, or Y, or Z. Anna.

She paused, then went on in a serious voice—Now I need for you to listen to me Sal, and to not interrupt or to ask any questions, okay?

I nodded.

This is the last time you're going to see me. I know you have a lot of questions. I know there are many things you want to understand. I'm going to give you something.

Anna walked over to where her coat was hanging and from an interior pocket produced a wad of folded-up pages.

Here, she said, and handed them to me.

This is what Jimmy had been working on before ... well, before you received his phone call. It was going to be a novel. Abyssinia. This was how far he'd gotten.

I want you to read it, Sal, and properly absorb and digest what is in there. Okay? Sometimes the only way to understand is through stories. The way in which we choose or are chosen to tell them. Why we tell them. Does that make sense?

I nodded, doing my best to not interrupt or ask a question.

Thanks for the dance, Salvo. And the Fanta.

Anna put on her coat and hat and gloves. Keaton stared up at her expectantly.

Ludwig, she said to him, maybe you can teach your friend Sal some lullabies, huh?

Silence from Keaton.

Stay curious, Salvo, Anna said, turned and was gone.

Run out into the hallway and say something to her, anything, screamed a voice in my head. Yet I remained still. For a while.

Fanta comes from the German word fanataise, which means imagination.

I wrote that down in my notebook. Then underneath:

As told to me by Anna.

IV

Dearest Isabelle,

The operation was performed yesterday. The Doctor, one of those self-satisfied idiots with a grin to match, declared it a success. Can you imagine that? Nine-tenths of my leg amputated and this butcher pats himself on the back while his harem of filthy nurses take turns jerking him off. I could go on about the follies that make up this Modern Medicine Show but will spare you the ramblings of an embittered invalid.

The doctor says I am cured. Whatever it was inside of me, eating me up, has been excised, and he expects I will make a full recovery and live a full and functional life as a one-legged gimp. Any carnivals hiring in your area? I am sorry. How are you? Are you and Martin getting on okay? How are the children? Please come visit me soon. I very much need to see you. Until then, my heart against yours.

Your brother, the Invalid

The letter, finished and sealed in an envelope, will go out with tomorrow's mail. It is the first letter Arturo has ever written to his sister, Isabelle. Not only has he never written to his sister, he has never written about her. He has written about nearly every other person, real and imagined, who's come into and out of his life, has written about every family member, real and imagined, but never, not once, has he written to or about his sister. Why is that, he wonders.

He knows that he is writing her because she knew him when he was young, as he knew her, and he couldn't write to his mother because she was dead, though, truth be told, even if she had been alive he wouldn't have written her—the matter of her death was an airtight alibi—and he never knew his father and there was the how and why of writing someone you don't know (though one time, many years ago, he drafted a letter to his father, as if he had known this man all along, and solidified the fantasy of his reality by tearing up the letter after it had been written, thinking—I can't send this to him. It will hurt him too much).

So he wrote to his sister, who knew him as a little boy, once.

The hospital bed on which Arturo lay, recovering, was a rusty steel-framed cot. Arturo's head was propped on two off-white pillows. The pillowcases smelled vaguely of plastic roses. This unsettled Arturo deeply, knowing that real roses give off a clean, slightly spiked scent and fake roses give off a cheap plastic scent. And so sniffing the pillowcases, a habit which Arturo had developed in the past week and showed no signs of breaking, bittersweetly reminded him that real roses reflected Nature and fake roses reflected Artifice, and the world could be divided that simply.

The blanket which covered Arturo was no blanket at all but a coarse burlap sack that scratched and irritated his skin. He didn't request a softer, genuine blanket because he wanted to begrudgingly savor and internalize the blemishes attached to the hospital. The hospital where they stole his leg was the same hospital where the pillowcases smelled of cheap plastic roses and the blanket was a coarse burlap sack that scratched and irritated his skin. He needed to despise this place as deeply as he could and remember it with only bitterness and disdain.

Arturo had been a poet, once upon a time, but that business had ended at nineteen. Or so it was said. If true, it is interesting to note that he stopped being a poet when he stopped being a teenager. That may or may not be pure coincidence. Historians cannot say if there's a significant connection between Arturo's renunciation of poetry and the loss of his youth.

As a poet, Arturo was best outlined by Plato's tiki-torch: "And a third kind of possession and madness comes from the Muses. This takes hold upon a gentle and pure soul, arouses it and inspires it to songs and other poetry, and thus by adorning countless deeds of the ancients educates later generations. But he who without the divine madness comes to the door of the Muses, confident that he will be a good poet by art, meets with no success, and the poetry of the sane man vanishes into nothingness before that of the inspired madmen."

Some time later. Arturo is asleep. He is groaning and writhing. There is both the pain from the absence of his leg and a nightmare. Nurse Fred, dressed in starched white, enters the room carrying a tray of unpalatable food. He sees that Arturo is groaning and writhing and wonders if he should interfere or allow whatever it was that had Arturo in its grip to run its course. He sets the tray on the table to the left of Arturo's bed. He whispers—Arturo, Arturo—wanting to wake him yet afraid to wake him. Arturo continues to writhe and groan. Arturo, he says louder, and lightly touches Arturo's shoulder.

A film of sweat flushes his forehead. Arturo opens his eyes and stares out blankly. He slowly turns to Fred, who registers as a foreign and inscrutable figure.

Who are you, Arturo asks.

Fred. I'm Nurse Fred. I think ... I think you might've been having a nightmare.

Nurse Fred smiles, as if the nightmare was a hospitable bond between nurse and patient.

I brought you food, Nurse Fred says.

Arturo looks at the tray and wrinkles his eyes. He sniffs his pillowcase and says: This place is nothing but cheap plastic roses. Your pillowcase, your food, all of it, cheap plastic roses.

I don't understand, Nurse Fred says.

Of course you don't Nurse Fred. You're not the one smelling and eating cheap plastic roses.

Nurse Fred nods, assuming it was the medication talking.

Where's ... what's the blonde's name?

Julie.

Yes, Julie. Where is she?

She'll be back in the morning.

Arturo looks away. Then he turns to Nurse Fred and signals: Come here, please.

Nurse Fred moves closer.

Closer, Arturo softly commands. And lean down.

Fred does as he is told. Arturo sniffs his neck.

Julie smells a lot better than you do. Julie smells like a sea breeze.

Arturo closes his eyes and imagines Julie and deeply inhales the sea breezy scent of her. Arturo opens his eyes and says: Julie's sea-breeze is of nature, Nurse Fred. Not artifice. Not cheap plastic roses that kill you slowly.

Arturo went on: Between you and me, Nurse Fred ... I'd like to fuck Julie. Could you possibly arrange that?

Arturo, I'm—

Not a pimp, yes Nurse Fred, I know and respect your official position in this whole thing. It's just ... they took away my left leg and left me with this unrelenting hard-on. I thought Julie, as a trained professional, might know some procedure.

Arturo, Fred says, your food is here if you'd like to eat. Is there anything else I can get you?

Aside from Nurse Julie? Let me think ... perhaps, a throat?

Excuse me?

Yes, could you bring me a throat? One throat to throttle ... or maybe cut. If I'm to cut it though, I'll need a knife. One knife and one throat please!

Nurse Fred shakes his head.

What is that look, Nurse Fred? Is that pity? Is that disgust? Are you, the two-legged little nurseboy, feeling sorry for the poor, suicidal, sex–crazed invalid? Perhaps you could loan me your flabby pink throat and I'll settle the score for both of us. Do you feel sorry for an invalid who is so bad off he's making outrageous requests for a throat and a knife?

I'm going, Nurse Fred says, and walks out.

Wait, Nurse Fred ... I want a glass of ... ah fuck it, stay

thirsty.

Arturo leans back on his pillows and stares at the ceiling. Like the smell of cheap plastic roses, the scarred complexion of the off-white ceiling disturbs Arturo, further indulging his hatred of the hospital.

Fractal #1, Arch, enters through the wall on the left, clapping loudly.

Bravo, that was quite a performance old man! We really gave it to Male Nurse Fred, didn't we?

Arturo ignores Arch and continues staring at the ceiling

Arch is thin and gaunt and there is a calcified severity to his movements and gestures. His eyes: a hard piercing blue clouded over by wisps of gray, and his face, sunbaked a reddish-ochre, set off the iciness of his eyes. He is dressed in baggy, beige, linen attire—what seems an ideal outfit for hot climates. He walks with a slightly exaggerated limp and a cigarette dangles from his lips.

Arch moves closer to the bed.

I am applauding your performance and you won't even acknowledge my presence.

Arturo slowly turns to Arch and says: Don't you mean our performance?

Well, yes, I suppose I do deserve some of the credit.

Arch picks up the empty glass from the table and stares into it. Thirsty?

Arturo doesn't answer.

Arch taps the glass repeatedly with his fingernail. I said ... are you thirsty?

Arturo remains silent and looks toward the window, trying to lose himself in the intersecting floral patterns embroidered on the pine-green curtains.

Arch continues: How do you like that ... they cut off his leg and his hearing goes too.

Arch walks to the sink, fills the glass halfway and sets it on the table.

Arturo continues to stare at or into the intersecting floral patterns, and suddenly the curtains are billowed by a dramatic whoosh, parting them like two torn capes, and through the open space emerges Fractal #2, Sophelia.

Sophelia is tall and willowy and dressed in a translucent pale gold gown. Her hair is the red of orgies and bled orchard fruits, and her skin is a preternatural white—as if she were dead and ceremonially preserved or prepared to play a geisha in a kabuki performance. The rest of her colors wash over Arturo in a stimulating mélange, and he, the synesthesiac, can taste them deeply: the violet of her fingernail paint, the lavender shading her eyes, the luster of her black knee-high combat boots.

Why don't you leave him alone, Sophelia says, quietly yet firmly, to Arch.

Arch claps loudly.

What an entrance! The damsel in a dress to the Invalid's rescue. Is this not the stuff that fairytales are made from?

Arturo gawks at Sophelia who stands by the window.

Sophelia, he says, what are you doing here?

I've been here the whole time Arturo.

I don't understand, you left—

After you put her over your knee, spanked her, cursed her, and kicked her pretty ass out. You had quite a temper in those days Arturo.

So ... you've come back?

I never left.

You weren't with me.

I was with you.

Arch says to Sophelia—Allow me, your Grace—then to Arturo—She was with you old man. Where would she have gone? Where would any of us go? Though I will admit, tracking the soul of a whore is no easy task.

Through the floor, directly under the cot, Fractal #3 ascends and the top of his head bumps the underside of the cot, which rattles. Curling himself up into a ball, he rolls out from the under the cot and springs to his feet, plastic sword in hand. He points the sword at Arch and says: You'd best curb your tongue and mind your manners, sir!

Arch smiles and issues a mock-welcoming gesture: As if on cue, his Travesty, the Brat Prince.

Fractal #3 is Icarus V. Dandywine.

Icarus V. Dandywine is shirtless and wearing a tattered black cape that appears to have been chewed through by a wild beast. Ash-marks and fresh pink scratches colonize his chest and arms. His sand-colored hair is thick and unruly. His pants, cotton pajama bottoms, are purple with thin horizontal green stripes. He is barefoot.

Icarus waves his sword at Arch. I've got half-a-mind to bash your skull in!

I'll see your half-a-mind and raise you a severed limb. Quick, Artie, where's your left leg?

Arch laughs a short cruel laugh. Icarus regards him with quiet burning contempt. Sophelia is staring softly at Arturo. Arturo notices and says: You've been with me the whole time?

Sophelia nods. Arturo gives Icarus a look and Icarus walks over to Sophelia and ducks his head into the crook of her shoulder. Sophelia runs her fingers through his mane and, watching, Arturo dreams of what it would feel like to be touched, a soft whimper escaping through his nostrils. Arch stubs out his cigarette on Arturo's food and quickly lights another one. He says to Arturo, indicating Icarus with the lighted end of his cigarette—Think somebody just lightened his load, eh?

Icarus raises and turns his head and stares at Arch, the tiger in his eyes prepared to pounce.

Sophelia says: Do you see what you've made Arturo?

Blame Nature, not Arturo, Arch says. I'm simply the time-hardened feces of this little shit.

Icarus shouts: You and I have nothing in common!

Which is exactly why I'm here today. And yesterday. And tomorrow. Should I go on?

I wish you wouldn't, Arturo says.

Of course you wish that, of course, Arch fires back.

Everyone is quiet and mostly still. Then Arch holds out a burnished copper cigarette case with the initials E.T.C.

engraved in the center. He flips open the lid and holds out the case to Arturo. Arturo doesn't reach for one.

Go on, they're hand-rolled, Arch says.

Arturo takes one and places it between his dry lips. Arch flips him a book of matches. Arturo is about to strike the match on the flint but his hand is trembling violently. Arch takes the match and lights the cigarette for Arturo.

Icarus tells Arturo: I wrote a song. Would you like to hear it?

Arch says: Let me guess ... a ballad ... about her.

Icarus ignores Arch. Arturo?

Yes, Icarus, let's hear it.

You'll have to imagine my sword's a guitar, okay?

While you're imaging things, Arch says to Arturo, imagine your whore's a Muse. For the sake of the ballad.

Icarus shouts: You don't know how to treat women!

Correction, Junior, Arch says, I don't know how to treat people. Women notwithstanding.

Icarus thrusts his sword forward as it extends like a bridge over the bed. Arch takes hold of its tip. There is a brief tug of war then Arch lets go and Icarus tumbles backward, flat on his ass. Arch laughs, again short and cruel. Then he says to Arturo: And this is who you chose to play your hero?

He's not a hero.

Icarus gets up and says: I AM a hero. Then he turns to Sophelia and softly asks: Am I not a hero?

Sophelia brushes the hair away from his forehead and says: Play us your song, Icarus.

Icarus nods and walks to the edge of the cot.

A guitar, okay, he says to Arturo.

Arturo nods.

Icarus holds his sword as he would a guitar. A concentrated spot of blue light encloses him. His sword transforms into a guitar one might see a troubadour playing in the 12th century.

Electric, he says to Arturo, and his 12th century guitar transforms into a black-and-white Fender. Icarus begins playing softly. A medieval sea-shanty. He sings in a shrill yet jagged warble:

Sophelia, Sophelia,
why so blue?
Has love, your lover,
found a darker shade of you?

Icarus looks at Sophelia, whom he now sees seated in a lush red lounge chair cast in a milky rose light.

The razors in Icarus' voice grow sharper:

Sophelia, Sophelia,
why so blue?
Has love, your lover,
found a darker shade of you?

And sharper still.

Sophelia, Sophelia,
why so blue?
Has love, your lover,
found a darker shade of you?

Arch, whom Icarus has reduced to a disembodied voice, says: Seems our balladeer is stuck on repeat.

Sophelia, Sophelia,
why so pure?
Does the answer
lie on a distant shore?

Sophelia, Sophelia,
I gave you my vow,
sealed it with a kiss
right before you drowned.

Icarus' razors reach a punk-edged pitch, raveled in the Fender's fuzz and barbed wire.

SOPHELIA SOPHELIA
SOPHELIA SOPHELIA
SOPHELIA SOPHELIA

And down to a trembling whisper.

Why so blue?

Everybody now, shouts Arch, and he sings along with Icarus.

Has love, your lover,
found a darker shade of you?

Icarus bows his head. He is dripping pools of sweat. He wipes at his eyes with the hem of his cape. The blue spot melts away, replaced by the hospital's sickly bronze tint. The Fender reverts back to a plastic sword. Icarus stares at Sophelia who is once again standing by the window. The tears in her throat do not rise, so she swallows hard, three times. Then she turns, parts the curtains, opens the window, and dives out headfirst. Icarus looks at Arturo. Arturo nods. Icarus goes to the window and also dives out headfirst, his chewed-through cape inflated by the wind. Arch stubs his cigarette out on Arturo's food.

I'm not that dramatic, he says. I'll go out the same way I came in.

Arch hums the melody to Sophelia's Blues and exits through the wall on the left.

Arturo is alone. He grabs the cup from the table and downs the water in one gulp. He sniffs the pillowcase and retreats within and finds everything dry and cold, hard earth in winter. He comes back out and stares at the ceiling, noting

that one of its scars is shaped like a bell. He sees it ringing
and hears tigers running over snow, running toward
something he cannot see.

V

When I was done reading Jimmy's pages, I read them again. And again. Then a fourth time. Anna's directive echoed in my mind: Properly absorb and digest what is in there.

I got up and unplugged the phone. To eliminate the possibility of another phone call urging me down another curious path. Now was not the time for action. Now was the time to idle and reflect.

I placed Jimmy's pages in a manila envelope and in black marker wrote—Abyssinia—on the envelope. Then I placed it in the bottom drawer of my desk.

I fixed myself a cup of Orange Pekoe (I was out of Smoky Russian) and sat down in my recliner—sipping, thinking.

Arturo. Who was a fictionalized incarnation of the 19th century French poet, Arthur Rimbaud. Rimbaud was one of Jimmy's heroes. Among his, as Jimmy would say, "golden collected." This was the term Jimmy used when we were kids, collecting. I'm collecting James Bond, Jimmy would say, and for the next week or so Jimmy was James Bond. He'd talk with a British accent, never leave his house without his cast-iron Walter PPK cap-gun, and ask for his drinks to be stirred and not shaken (especially strange since the request was being made of the counter-guy at Angelo's Pizza who'd be serving Jimmy a fountain Coke).

Jimmy's adoption of characters was intense and mercurial. His passion for and absorption in, let's say Luke Skywalker, would be singular and fanatical, then Bruce Lee or the Green Hornet would claim his affections and Skywalker was dropped and forgotten. In this way Jimmy cycled through a multitude of personas.

If I had to pick a specific moment that best defined Jimmy's relationship with collecting it would be that time in

117

the schoolyard, hanging out with friends, when Jimmy pulled me aside and said—Salvo, I've got something to tell you.

There was a gravity in Jimmy's voice that made me think he was about to confess a crime or dark family secret.

What I'm about to tell you is gonna sound crazy, but it's true and you can't tell another soul. Promise?

I promised.

Jimmy took a deep breath then said—I'm Spider-Man.

The urge to laugh in Jimmy's face was muted by the awe that I felt for the conviction with which Jimmy had made his statement. Jimmy wasn't pretending, he was believing. And so, without realizing what I was doing, I honored Jimmy's belief by assuring him—Your secret's safe with me.

As Jimmy grew up his tastes in collecting changed to reflect the changes in his needs and desires. Super-heroes and crime-fighters were replaced by writers. Jack Kerouac, Henry Miller, Ernest Hemingway, William Faulkner, Scott Fitzgerald, William Saroyan, Dylan Thomas—these and other writers became mythical personas which Jimmy both found and lost himself in. Rimbaud ranked as one of Jimmy's "golden collected" because he was one of the ones with whom Jimmy felt a unique kinship.

Rimbaud's famous line—"Je ust un autre" ("I is another")—was one of Jimmy's mantras, and he always talked about writing something—a story, a novel, a play—that really captured the Rimbaudedness of Rimbaud.

Now I was in possession of six handwritten pages starring Arturo who was Arthur Rimbaud who was Jimmy Barrone. It was psychic incest, Jimmy-style, but what of it? That was something Jimmy had been doing his whole life. Maybe Jimmy had a diagnosable disorder, maybe he didn't. Maybe Jimmy was simply a crazy writer who drank too much and imagined too vividly. In that respect Jimmy was not exceptional. In fact when it came to writers it was an almost unforgivable cliché.

I started to feel pissed off at Jimmy and his crazymaking. Why the fuck had he called me? We hadn't talked in years and out of nowhere I'm the one he drops his existential shit-bomb on. Fuck you, Jimmy Barrone. Fuck you and your crazymaking.

I felt anxious and didn't want to think about Jimmy Barrone or his pages anymore. I paced around my apartment, detesting every inch of it.

You're small and ugly and stupid, I screamed at it, as if it were a child that I wanted to crush. I grabbed a kitchen chair and smashed it against the edge of the kitchen sink. I kept smashing it until the chair was mostly splinters. I flung its last solid leg against the window, which shattered and fell both inward and streetside, along with the leg. Arturo's leg, I thought, before breathing in a chilling wind.

There's nothing quite like a blast of cold air to return a person to their right and sober state of mind. I was suddenly aware that not only was I an idiot, I was also an idiot who didn't have enough money to buy a new window. The chances of my tightwad landlady replacing the window were zero to none. I could hear her ratchety Sicilian dialect now—Sal-a, why you need a new weendow, joost put-a Saran Wrap, you be fine.

I blankly stared at the shards of glass on the floor. Then out the glassless window. My mind struggled to reconcile the two. The cold wasted no time in its hostile takeover of my apartment. I put on a sweat-jacket and swept up the shards of glass. Then I swept up the puddle of splinters.

When I was done I started dialing Tania's work number then stopped and hung up. I got out the Yellow Pages and found the number for The Diving Mermaid. I called.

Diving Mermaid, came the voice that sounded like Frank's.

I asked if Hen was around—this is Sal—to which the voice responded—Hold the line. Several seconds later Hen's voice exploded through the line.

After a lengthy preamble I asked Hen if I could borrow money to have my window fixed. Hen said it was no problem—Come down to the Mermaid and I'll get you squared.

I spent the next twenty minutes taping together all the plastic bags I had and rehung a poor man's window. I stood and waited to see what would happen. The windowbag ruffled and ballooned but didn't come down as the air like cold fists punched against it. Satisfied, I grabbed the envelope with Jimmy's pages in it and left.

By time I got to the Mermaid it was happy hour and the place was buzzing. Frank had put up an artificial Christmas tree adjacent to the jukebox. The tree was white and strung up with flickering red and blue lights.

Hen said we'd drink a couple of rounds, his treat, then head over to his place so he could show me his artwork.

Here, I said, and handed Hen the manila envelope.

What's this?

I started to give Hen the lowdown but once he heard that the pages had come from Anna, and that she had been at my apartment, his eyes bulged and he cut me off—Waitwaitwait Anna was at your place   you got to bed down a goddess you lucky faun you   if I were you I wouldn't wash my dick neverever   don't wash away goddessjuice stains   unless you already have have you.

I explained that I had not stained myself with goddessjuice, that Anna and I had mostly talked and slow-danced a little.

Hen jammed his thumb against his forehead, repeatedly, and bemoaned—Sal Sal Sal Sal Sal   Anna comes back to your place slowdances with you and   oh man   this lady wanted you all of you inside her   the father the son the holy spirit amen and then some   SHE WANTED YOU.

I smiled and said nothing. It was nice to entertain Hen's illusion that Anna had wanted me. The father, the son, the holy spirit, amen and then some. Not true but nice to think so.

I changed the subject back to Jimmy's pages. It was going to be a novel, I said. Titled Abyssinia. Based on Arthur

Rimbaud.

Hen broke into an asthmatic laugh while slapping his palm against the edge of the counter. Then he took a hearty swig of his stout before reciting:

> Perhaps there's an evening in store
> Where I'll drink quietly
> In some old city
> And die the happier—
> Patient as I am!
> If my affliction ever lets up
> If I ever come by gold
> Will I choose the North
> Or vineyard country?
> Ah dreaming is shameful
> A perfect form of loss
> And if I become once more
> The Traveller I was
> The Green Inn will have barred its door.

A smattering of applause broke out around us. One man clapped Hen on the back and said—Wuzzat Shakespeare?

No Rimbaud, Hen replied. The Comedy of Thirst.

Rambo, came the raised eyebrows in the man's voice. You mean Sly Stallone Rambo?

Hen stared at the guy with a barbed twinkle in his eye and said nothing. Then: Yea Sly Stallone   poet of the streets of the people voice of our generation.

Hen and I drank one more round and left.

Hen lived in a basement apartment of an old brownstone.   He said that the woman who owned the brownstone and lived upstairs was an old blind widow with lots of cats.

Lady Gray that's what I call her Lady Gray   she's cut from golden cloth   me and her sometimes sit up late and drink sherry and talk   I help her around the house run errands for her   she lets me use the shed in the back as my studio   Lady Gray's my best critic runs her fingers over my paintings and if something's missing   if she don't feel the soul or fire or whatever she tells me   she feels my paintings and when she don't feel em I know I've failed   back to the drawing board y'know.

Hen's apartment was colonized by paintings. They took up every inch of wall space, and the ones that hadn't found a home on the wall lay in fugitive stacks and piles set on the floor, or against the few pieces of furniture he owned. Yet according to Hen every painting was exactly where it should be.

All the paintings that belong together, Hen explained, are together   not one is living with the wrong family.

As Hen played docent to my tourist, I found that there were six categories, or families as Hen called them, into which one of his paintings could fall.

Cubist Porn (erotic images and body parts that had been radically reconfigured)

Spare Me the Details (Sumi-e-style works done in calligraphy)

Mermaid Parade (images reflecting Coney Island, mostly done in oils)

Bodega Blues (a series devoted to urban neighborhood scenes with blue being the predominant color)

White Noise for the Color Blind (paintings with thick white backgrounds and black squiggle lines, dots and hyphens that formed a concert of movement)

Baron Fields (ultra-colorful paintings that cast modern celebrities and cultural figures in historical and mythical settings)

When I expressed to Hen how much I loved one of the pictures from the Mermaid Parade family—in which a solitary woman is standing on the boardwalk, her back turned to the viewer, staring out at the thousands of people on the beach, who appear as blurred specks—he said: That one's called Mara take her she's yours.

No Hen, I started but Hen thrust the unframed painting, about 11x16, into my hands and insisted that I take her.

I looked at Mara looking at the people who looked nothing like people. The sea in the background was turquoise and nickel-plated.

Thank you Hen, I said. Do you show your work?

Yea yea I show, Hen said as if brushing away flies. Got gallery representation in the Village other places too I do okay but when I'm done with the painting I'm done with the painting know what I mean.

Seeing the number of paintings that took up residence in Hen's apartment, his statement seemed incongruous.

Hen continued—It's all part of one big unfinished Sal just variations on the same big unfinished know what I mean I love all my paintings for who they are but also for who they're not   the big question is do they love me back   I'll never know cuz they don't talk to me   don't say Hen we love you for who you are and who you're not or we could never love someone like you   never say a word that's the way I like it.

Hen got quiet for a moment then clapped his hands together and said—Time for some wine   I got a nice Bordeaux the other day   sixteen years old   people wait for special occasions   any occasion's a special occasion when you drink a nice Bordeaux   I should be writing wine commercials huh.

I sat in a frayed wicker chair and Hen sat on a stack of tires—covered by a sheet—that functioned as a chair. We talked and drank until there was no more Bordeaux, then Hen suggested we take the party upstairs to Lady Gray's.

If Hen's apartment was a gallery, Lady Gray's was a kennel inundated with feline odors and stray hairs. There must have been about twenty cats who greeted us with a cacophony of meows. Lady Gray was a spindly old woman with steel-gray hair and a small rusty voice. The skin covering her face and arms seemed like flesh-colored tissue paper that was susceptible to disintegration. Lady Gray's unseeing eyes were a remarkable blue that gave off strong light in an otherwise dark house.

As if sensing my thoughts, Lady Gray said—Dark, light, makes no difference to me, at least not in the cosmetic sense.

Lady Gray gave a short laugh then—Henry, turn on some lights so you boys can see. And pour us all some sherry.

The three of us drank sherry and talked. I noticed that Hen's bawdy nature was toned down around Lady Gray. At times he referred to her as Marm, and she referred to him as Sonnyboy.

I know my Sonnyboy, Lady Gray said, almost as if Hen weren't in the room—I know he's got some wicked ways. But I can feel him, his soul, in those paintings he does. His soul is not a wicked soul. It's a beautiful soul. But you know what—Lady Gray's voice went down to a conspiratorial whisper as she tapped her forefinger against her nose—Sonnyboy likes his drink a little too much.

I could tell that Hen enjoyed Lady Gray's gentle chastisement. I could also see in his eyes that he loved her. Maybe in a way that he didn't love anyone else.

At one point Hen told me to give my hand to Lady Gray.

Let Marm feel your hand   she says hands are the true windows to the soul not the eyes   right Marm?

Lady Gray smiled like a proud teacher whose student has learned well.

Give me your hand, Lady Gray softly commanded.

I gave Lady Gray my left hand. Her fingers, gaunt and tissue-skinned, explored my hand. I closed my eyes thinking this would somehow help her to feel me better. After about ten seconds she let her hand rest on top of mine, gloving it.

You have an extremely sensitive nature, she said. Too sensitive, I fear, for this world.

Know any other worlds where I can go, I cracked.

Yes, she said, but there's no guarantee that it will be any easier.

Then me and my sensitive nature will have to tough it out, huh?

Lady Gray smiled and nodded. Then, as she let go of my hand—Also, you've got very poor circulation in those hands, young man. Your hands are colder than mine and I'm almost two hundred years old. Try cold showers.

That night I went home with Mara, money for a new window, and an extra $100 that Hen had insisted on giving me as a Christmas gift.

Inside my apartment it was freezing. My bag-window had become a play-mate for Keaton, who was engaged in a wrestling match with it on the floor. Keaton and the bag were locked in a stalemate so I let their bout continue and did what I stupidly didn't think to do in the first place. I got an old quilt out of the closet and nailed it up as insulation.

I was out of tea so I made myself a cup of hot water with sugar. To stay warm I put on thermals, an extra pair of socks and my sweat-jacket. Then I sat in my recliner and studied my hands under the lamplight. I smoothed the fingertips of my left hand over the palm of my right. Soft, uncalloused, cold. I clicked on the TV.

While channel-surfing I came across the commercial for Ghostwriters, Inc. There was the sandy-haired Howell Downs. Confident, handsome, self-assured. He had a smile that sublimely broadcast—Trust me ... Trust me ... Trust me.

I missed ghosting but I wasn't so sure I would do it again, even if I had the means. Something about it had made me feel unreal. Not myself. Or was it that I had felt too much myself?

What about Jimmy, I wondered. Had he traveled a distance so deep inside himself, for so long, that he wound up ... where exactly? Or maybe who exactly was the better question.

The Trust-me smile of Howell Downs went off in my mind like a sinister flashbulb. I decided to follow Lady Gray's advice   and   went   to   take   a   cold   shower.

VI

I spent Christmas Eve at Rico and Desiree's. Having lifted my childish ban on Tania, of which she had been unaware, I spent Christmas day at her mother's house, where myself, Tania, her mother, and several of their relatives enjoyed a traditional Russian feast. I spent New Year's Eve at home, with my new window and Keaton, watching The Twilight Zone marathon. All in all it had been a pleasant holiday run until New Year's Day, when I received two phone calls that were the equivalent of storm-clouds.

The first call, from my landlady, I had been expecting.

Sal-a, happy New Year and don't forget to bring-a the rent by today, okay?

The second phone call, from Hen, was unexpected.

Jimmy's dead Sal   it's in the newspaper   jumped off the roof of his high-rise   poor fucker did himself in.

I went into the hallway to check on the availability of my neighbor's Daily News, but he had already picked it up. I rushed down to the bagel store, bought a paper, then sat on a crate outside the store and skimmed the pages until I found it.

Man Plunges to Death off Coney Island High-Rise

The story came to me in isolated fragments.

Jimmy Barrone.   Writer. Age thirty-one.   Apparent suicide. No suicide note.

Then the line that chilled me—The impact from the fall had smashed Barrone beyond recognition.

A photo of Jimmy accompanied the article. It was the one that had appeared on the sleeve-jacket of Milking the Elephant. Jimmy was standing, wearing a fedora at a rakishly tilted angle, hands in his pockets. The photo reflected a solid and sturdy-looking man, not someone who would wind up broken and smashed beyond recognition.

Three days later, Jimmy's funeral was held at DiPietro's in Bensonhurst. It was the same place where both of our mother's funerals had been held.

I arrived with Tania, Rico and Desiree, and as expected the funeral doubled as a reunion. A lot of people I had grown up with and hadn't seen in years were in attendance. As were Jimmy's relatives, and several of his ex-girlfriends. There was a small contingent I recognized from the Mermaid, including Hen and Frank. Anna wasn't there. Even though she told me I wouldn't see her anymore, I hoped that she might show up to pay her last respects.

Jimmy's body had been cremated, and in place of a coffin there was an altar. Photos of Jimmy, at different ages, were the centerpiece of the altar, which was surrounded by flowers. All of them, as far as I could tell, were real.

The priest, a stoop-shouldered fossil of a man, delivered a eulogy that was dry and prescriptive. It contained the usual company-line about Jimmy finding the peace in heaven that he hadn't found on earth, and becoming one with Our Father, the Lord.

I thought about my ghost, Y., and its afterlife in a no-man's-land of cold.

This priest is a fucking idiot, I hiss-whispered to Tania, who was sitting next to me. She responded by firmly squeezing my hand.

The priest did close with something that rang true to Jimmy's character.

And let us take into our hearts, this passage, which James Joseph Barrone held in the highest regard ... the words of Jesus as given to us by his disciple, Matthew—Truly, I say to you, unless you are converted and become as little children, you will by no means enter the kingdom of Heaven.

After the eulogy people took turns visiting the altar. The

mood in the room was subdued, with a pervasive sense of—I can't believe it—bristling in the air. The only dramatic outburst came from Jimmy's Uncle Gianni. While kneeling before the altar he began shaking uncontrollably, and shouted—Why, why did you this to yourself Jimmy, what's wrong with you—and kept on until his wife, Marie, came over and gently guided him away. Tania, whose arm was locked inside mine, began trembling and with tears in her voice said—Why did he do it—picking up the thread of inquiry that Uncle Gianni had left dangling.

I went to the altar and kneeled before it. I laid the rosary beads I had stolen from Jimmy's apartment in front of a photo of young Jimmy. I stared at young Jimmy and couldn't decide whether the look in his eyes was one of secret joy or hidden hurt. Or if there was even a difference.

It seemed that except for Hen, myself and the contingent at the Mermaid, no one knew that Jimmy had gone to North Carolina. And none of the newspapers had mentioned Jimmy having recently returned from a trip. Had Jimmy gone to North Carolina? If so, what had happened there?

I needed air and went outside where Hen joined me. He and I shared nips of whiskey from the flask he had brought with him. It suddenly struck me, in an awful way, that the suit Hen was dressed in was the same size suit that a young boy would wear.

The whole thing stinks, Hen said. Fucking Jimmy.

Fucking Jimmy, I repeated without much conviction.

No I mean the whole thing's all wrong, Hen went on. You got Jimmy's funeral but no Jimmy and in place of Jimmy you got a photo collection what the fuck is that I don't like it guy doesn't even have the courtesy to show up for his own funeral ballbuster he is.

Ballbuster he was, I corrected Hen.

We both started laughing hysterically, and in the spaces between our laughter we squeezed in—Fucking Jimmy this and fucking Jimmy that.

Once we stopped laughing Hen suggested we go to the

Mermaid and honor Jimmy's memory in a way that Jimmy would have truly appreciated—with booze and storytelling.

After I said good-bye to Tania, Rico dropped off Desiree, then the three of us—me, Hen and Rico—drove to the Mermaid. On the drive over Rico pumped The Beastie Boy's Licensed to Ill as a tribute to Jimmy. In the rearview I saw Hen bopping and squirming in his seat like a child on the verge of wetting himself.

By the time we got to the Mermaid it was dark. It was a Wednesday and the place was about half-full. Frank and several of the others who had been at the funeral were back at the bar. I saw that the white Christmas tree was still up, as were the other holiday decorations.

Me, Hen and Rico got a table and Hen told us that he'd cover all our drinks.

Drink as much as you want to, Hen said, for Jimmy.

Which became our alibi and refrain throughout the night.

Let's do shots. For Jimmy. Let's cut up some of Rico's pills and snort them. For Jimmy. Let's play these songs on the jukebox. For Jimmy.

Everything was for and about Jimmy until it wasn't.

Hen grew carnivorously lustful and let the women around him know. Rico rapped to himself with insular conviction. I became locked inside a hateful silence.

Then I found the man that I needed. A bald guy with a kiss-print tattoo, seated at the bar. Instantly I tagged him as both my enemy and an insidious force that had to be stopped. My innate hatred of Kissprint was externally justified when I saw him mercilessly hitting on the girl seated next to him. She needs me, I thought. To rescue her, and to make things right.

I shot up from my seat, went to the bar, and aggressively slotted myself between the two of them. Then I looked Kissprint square in the eye and mumbled some incoherent one-liner, more Rambo than Rimbaud.

The phantom punch connected and I was on the floor so

fast it was as if I had been there all along. I stared up at the ceiling, which looked diffuse and foggy. A lot of commotion took place around me and the noise level of the bar rose dramatically.

Two guys helped me to my feet. I leaned against the bar to steady myself. I saw that Kissprint was laid out on the floor, several feet away. Rico was frantically waving his hand, saying—Think I broke my hand on the fucker's head.

Hen was still seated and still drinking. He looked quietly amused. He pointed at me and shouted—Check your bill, platypus.

I ran my fingers over my mouth. Blood.

I went to the bathroom and inspected my face in the mirror. My upper lip was cartoonishly inflated and moist with blood. I rinsed off the blood then noticed that one of my front teeth was chipped. What formerly had been a smooth and even edge was now jagged.

When I returned to the bar Kissprint was gone. Apparently he had come to and stumbled out without saying a word. Rico was now seated at the table with Hen, icing his hand. I joined them.

Fucker had a hard head, Rico said and gave a small laugh.

You think it's broken, I said.

His head?

No your hand.

Nah, I don't think so, Rico said, removing the ice pack and wiggling his fingers. His hand was bright pink and badly swollen.

I looked around and didn't see her.

What happened to the girl, I asked.

What girl, Rico said.

The girl I was trying to save.

What the fuck are you on about, Hen said.

I looked at the both of them looking at me. I suddenly grew tired and lost interest.

Never mind, I said.

Frank came over, handed me an ice-pack and asked if I

was alright.

Fine, I said, pressing the ice pack against my mouth.

That was some punch, Frank said to Rico and smiled. Whaddya drinking?

Alize, Rico said.

Coming up.

I could've told you this was gonna happen, Hen said to me and laughed. I knew that you wanted bad to happen needed it could see it in your eyes.

My eyes, I said, but the hands are the windows to the soul, Hen, remember?

What the fuck are you two talking about, Rico said.

Nothing Rico, I said.

Hen lifted his mug and chanted—Our Fodder who art ain't nothing hallow be-bop-a-lula my name is nada nada nada zip nil zilch amen & nevermore THE END.

Rico and I left Hen at the Mermaid. We sat in Rico's parked car listening to the Wu-Tang Clan. Rico cut up some more pills and snorted several lines. For my hand, he explained and smiled.

He passed me the credit card on which the lines were laid and said—Doctor's orders. I snorted several lines.

When we started driving I suddenly realized where I needed to go.

Drop me at the train station, Rico, I said.

Where you going, he asked.

Tania's.

Rico laughed. You think that's a good idea?

I don't know, I said.

Sal-fucking-eeee, Rico said, and punched me in the arm with his good hand.

Showing up at Tania's turned out to be a bad idea.

Things started off promising when Tania answered the door in a pale blue nightgown, the scent of warm sleep coming off her body.

Sal, she said, her eyes adjusting to the light she had just turned on. What are you doing here?

I stepped from the pitch-black of her hallway into the light of her studio.

Ohmigod, your mouth, she said. What happened?

Fight, I said, making sure to sound extra-nonchalant. But I'm fine. And I come bearing cheap whiskey.

I slid the pint of Evan Williams I had bought out of a brown bag.

I know it's late and I should have called but. I just couldn't go home.

Yea, Tania said, then—yea—again, this time in a different voice. The second yea alerted me. I looked over Tania's shoulder and saw a dark-haired man splayed stomach-down on her bed, which was situated in the far corner of the studio.

Oh, I said, I'm sorry.

No-no, it's alright. Come in. It's. That's Teddy, my friend Teddy that I told you about.

Friend Teddy was no longer just a term but a physical presence visible in Tania's bed. One that was slowly coming to life as he turned over, sat up and faced the two of us.

Hey, he said in a fuzzy voice.

I didn't know if the hey was meant for me or for Tania. I kept quiet and ran my tongue over the jagged edge of my chipped tooth.

Teddy, Tania said, taking me by the arm and leading me forward, this is my friend Sal. He's. It's been a rough night. He got into a fight. What exactly happened, Tania said, turning to me.

Teddy rose from the bed and knuckled the sleep out of his eyes. He was wearing boxers and nothing else. His apparatus swung freely, drawing attention to its existence. I wondered how long it had been since he had been inside Tania, and how long it had lasted.

Sal, Tania urged, what happened?

I stared at Tania, mostly not comprehending her as a

person. She wasn't wearing glasses and her cheeks were puffy from sleep. They could have been fucking ten minutes ago, twenty minutes, an hour. There was no way to know.

I looked at Tania, then at Teddy, then settled on the clock on the wall and began telling my story.

What happened. We were at the bar and this guy, some asshole with a kiss-print tattoo on his neck, insulted my friend Hen. Hen's a dwarf, I explained to Teddy, and this guy called Hen a dirty midget. So I got in the guy's face and said—You should learn the difference between a dwarf and a midget, fuckface. That's when the guy nailed me in the mouth.

Oh Sal, Tania said, sympathy cracking her voice. That looks pretty bad. Are you okay?

Yea-yea I'm fine. Look I got this too, I said, and opened my mouth to show Tania and Teddy my chipped tooth. Teddy moved in closer.

Oh man, he said. That's why I don't even like to go out to the bars anymore. Too many drunks looking for trouble, you know.

Tell me about it, I agreed emphatically.

I held up the pint of Evan Williams and said—How about a nightcap Teddy? Tania? T & T. Did you know that together you're T & T?

Teddy grinned a boyish grin and slipped his beefy arm around Tania's waist.

Let's celebrate love, I practically shouted. Love and death. Wasn't it Keats who said those were the only two things worth writing about? Or was it Yeats? I always get my Yeats and Keats confused.

I tore the seal off the bottle and Tania set down two glasses loaded with ice.

I'm not drinking, she said and yawned. I have to be up at seven tomorrow.

More for me and Teddy, right Ted?

Think I'll go easy myself, he said.

Tell me when, I said, as I poured the whiskey over the ice, which made a delayed cracking sound.

When, Teddy said, his glass about half-full. I poured myself a slightly larger amount.

I looked at Tania and said—I'm sorry for barging in on you guys like this. It's late and I didn't call.

I turned to Teddy—You see, my friend, well more like my brother, killed himself several days ago. The funeral was today.

I know, Teddy spoke in a quiet voice. Tania told me. I'm sorry.

Yea it's. Well it is what it is.

I sipped my drink. Then—What did you think of the funeral Tania?

What did I think of it?

Yea all things considered.

I'm not even sure what that means. It was really really sad. Especially when Jimmy's Uncle lost it.

She explained to Teddy—Jimmy's uncle was crying and shaking and kept shouting—Why did you do it? It broke my heart.

Tania turned back to me and said—Why do you think he did it?

You asked me that earlier, T.

I know and you didn't say anything.

I didn't say anything because I have no fucking idea.

Is that true, Tania pushed.

Is it true, I responded sharply. Does it matter? Does it matter if I have no idea or lots of ideas why Jimmy Barrone might have killed himself? What the fuck does it matter? He was bi-polar. He was a drunk. His father was a piece of shit. He thought the world was a terrible place. His hands were too sensitive. All of the above. None of the above. How the fuck do I know why people do the things they do? Jimmy Barrone took a dive off the roof of his building. SPLAT. End of story. That's what I know Tania.

I was now standing and my legs were trembling. I drank down the whiskey. I looked at Tania then Teddy. I couldn't read the expressions on their faces.

I'm sorry, I said quietly, I shouldn't have come here. I'm sorry Teddy, I said and extended my hand. If I were dating someone and some drunken idiot with a fucked-up mouth shows up at one in the morning and. And. Anyway I'm sorry. Tania's a good girl. She's the best. I'm sure you know that. I. FUCK. I'm sorry.

I began pacing around the studio, picking up and putting down objects. I needed to touch things, to hold them. Tania and Teddy both remained seated, and silent. I paced, picked up, put down. Paced, picked up, put down.

This went on for a while, then Tania rose from her chair.

Placed her body between me and the next object I was about to pick up.

And hugged me.

I buried my face in her shoulder, which I wanted to bite. Or gnash. Instead I found myself yielding to its support and began sobbing.

It's okay Sal, Tania kept repeating in a soft voice, it's okay.

That, and Tania's refusal to let go of me, allowed me to break down without coming apart.

It was about twenty minutes later when Teddy told Tania that I should spend the night and that he would go home. Tania said it was fine for all three of us to stay, she'd make up a bed on the floor. Before Teddy could say anything else, I rose from the chair I was sitting in and said that I was fine and needed to go. I needed to get home and that was all there was to it and thank you for everything.

I just need to use the bathroom before I go, I said.

I went to the bathroom and brushed my teeth. Then I gargled with Tania's generic brand of mint mouthwash. I studied my face in the mirror. The fat lip. The jagged tooth. The bags under my eyes.

You're a mess, I said, and stuck my tongue out at the mess staring back at me.

Then my attention caught on the pile of dirty clothes that

were on the floor next to the hamper. Without thinking about it too much I went through the dirty clothes and found four pairs of panties. I chose the pair that smelled most strongly of Tania and stuffed them in my pocket. For future reference.

VII

The days hadn't warmed up yet, but spring was right around the corner.

This was substantiated by the fact that pitchers and catchers had reported to camp. It didn't matter if it was barely above freezing, which it presently was, I measured the arrival of spring not by degrees or dates but by baseball.

I read the Daily News' previews of the Yankees and Mets while riding the subway home from work. About a month earlier I had gotten a job as a file clerk at an architecture firm in midtown. At Jimmy's funeral I had bumped into Rosario, a guy I had grown up with, and he'd given me the lead which had panned out. The pay wasn't great but the working conditions were favorable. I sat in a small room, by myself, and listened to my walkman while cataloguing the firm's never-ending stream of paperwork. Occasionally I ran errands.

My job in the real world allowed me to fix my tooth, plus I was catching up on rent. To buy time I'd told my landlady that I had written a book which had been accepted for publication and soon I'd be receiving a big advance. That bit of fiction, and the reminder that she and I were both Italian, had earned me a temporary reprieve.

One evening after work I met Tania at the Golden Dragon for dinner. We had only hung out once, taking in a Fellini double-feature, since that night at her house. We chatted with our usual ease and familiarity, and when the topic of Teddy came up Tania became both shy and excited.

What, I asked.

Well, she said, clenching a bit of lower lip between her teeth, Teddy's moving in. We're gonna live together.

Wow, I said, genuinely surprised. That's big. Isn't it?

Yes, my god, yes it's big. For me. You know how I am about my space. But it feels right, so. Why not?

That's great, T, really it is. We need more why-nots in the world. I'm happy for you, I said, and realized that for the most part I meant it.

Several minutes later Tania changed the subject to my personal life.

Whatever happened to Anna, she asked. Is that still going on?

No, I said, that's over. Anna left.

Oh. Is that a good thing, a bad thing?

I don't know, I said. She went back to Iceland. That's where she's originally from. She told me if I was ever in Iceland to look her up.

Tania leaned forward, smiled, and asked—Any plans to go to Iceland?

Maybe, I said, and smiled back. Why not, right?

I never did see Anna again, but two weeks later, I heard from her.

It was a Thursday night and I'd just gotten back from the Mermaid, where I hadn't been in a while. I was trying to cut down on my drinking and wanted to avoid the temptation of Hen's generosity. That night, though, it was Hen's fortieth birthday and he told me that he'd be gravely insulted if I didn't drop by to honor and affirm his existence.

I drank, but didn't get hammered, and found an opportune time to slip out when Josie put Hen over her lap and announced that, as a gift, she was going to spank him forty times.

When I got home, there it was, lying on the mat outside my door. A black tape recorder. It was identical to the one I had found at Jimmy's, not only in make but in the pink Post-It note attached to it, which read—Listen Up!

I took the recorder inside, fixed myself a cup of Smoky Russian and sat down on my recliner, the recorder in my lap. I tried to brace myself internally for whatever I was about to hear, then clicked the PLAY button.

Several seconds of dead air, followed by Anna singing Byssan Lull.

When she was done singing, Anna said:

Thought it best to start with a lullaby. That's the first time I've ever sung into a recorder. Hopefully it came across okay.

How are you Salvo? This is Anna. You're probably surprised to hear from me. As you should be. I shouldn't be doing this, just like I shouldn't have done some of the other things that I've done. Oh well. My deviant nature, I suppose.

Anyway, I think that if you're going to rebel and break rules, then you must look for angles. This, for instance. This is not me telling you all this right now, it's a recording of me. Not me. That's my angle.

What did you think of Abyssinia? Well what you thought of it is not the important thing. I gave you Abyssinia because ... let's say Abyssinia was a peephole. One that gives you a glimpse of something but also refracts and distorts the thing that you're glimpsing. Still talking in riddles, aren't I? I know, I'm a real stinker that way.

Okay, how about this. Question: Who was Sophelia? Answer: Me.

Refracted and distorted, with different color hair and those awful combat boots, but in the most essential sense—I am she.

You see, Salvo, I am Jimmy's muse. I was Jimmy's muse. That's what I am—a Muse.

The angels are white burning white and the eye that insists on confronting them shrivels.

Pretty scary, huh? All in good fun, though, Salvo, all in good fun.

So, yea, I shouldn't be telling you any of this. This is against our laws, as are all direct tamperings with mortal affairs. You know what Muses do? We inspire. That's all. Nothing more, nothing less. Yet myself, and other Muses, started to question—Is that all we're meant to do? Like humans, don't we have a choice? Aren't we allowed to choose different roles, ones that are less singular, if we really want to?

Like I said, deviant. That's me. Which, many would argue, is not a trait you want your Muse to possess.

That I manifested and walked your streets and saw your shows and drank your orange soda: against our laws. I'm certain there are going to be consequences for my actions—what those will be I have no idea. I don't care. What is it the humans like to say? You only live once. Not true, but still a great saying.

Do I in some way feel responsible for what happened to Jimmy? Perhaps, yes. Maybe that's why I made this recording.

You see, Salvo, I divorced myself from Jimmy a while back, when I no longer wanted to serve as a Muse. Times have changed and many Muses have revolted against the classic tradition for their own respective reasons. Is the relationship between Muses and humans in crisis? That I can't say for sure. What I will say, though—the connection has been compromised. On both sides.

You know as well I do, Jimmy was an exceptionally sensitive human being, and my absence in his life was a great loss for him.

Did Jimmy know that he had lost his Muse? No.

Did Jimmy know that he had lost his Muse? Yes.

On one level, what you humans like to call subconscious, Jimmy knew. He couldn't sit down and tell you—Salvo, I lost my Muse, Anna, who was tall with dark hair and white skin. A physical explanation, a conscious one—it wouldn't have happened that way.

And even though I thought I had divorced myself from Jimmy, really I hadn't. The bond between us turned out to be much stronger than I had imagined. Same as the bond that Jimmy shared with Laura Ciccerone. Laura was Jimmy's earth-Muse. I was Jimmy's ether-Muse.

While my sole function was to provide Jimmy with inspiration, Laura could have done and been so much more than that. Jimmy and Laura had the opportunity to become lovers, in a very real and very human way. They had the opportunity to create a life together. None of that happened, of course, but those possibilities existed for the both of them.

Something else you should know about Laura Ciccerone. She's dead. She died last October in North Carolina. A car crash. For a brief time she was in a coma, between worlds, and that was when she came to Jimmy in a dream. Or rather the story, which would have been born of Laura—Laura Ciccerone's Nightstand—came to Jimmy in a dream. Jimmy never heard about Laura's death, but if he would have written that story—it would have been his way of both honoring her life and grieving her death.

When Jimmy started ghosting, I was worried. Not because I think ghosting is bad. I don't really know much about it. I imagine that the humans turned to ghosting, and other shortcuts, to compensate for their disconnect from the Muses. That's perfectly understandable. Yet my fear was that ghosting would take Jimmy too far inward. In ways that were degenerate and unnatural.

You have to realize, Salvo, most humans only understand or perceive breakdowns in a very cosmetic and superficial way. There's a complexity there that's ... let me put it this way.

The Jimmy who went to North Carolina to find Laura Ciccerone is not the same Jimmy who called you. Nor are either one of them the seven-year-old Jimmy who is trying to find his way home. When a psychic splitting occurs, the fragments of self wander around—each with their own level of consciousness, each compelled by their own specific needs and desires. Which is why seven-year-old Jimmy won't stop trying to get home. Why North Carolina Jimmy will keep looking for Laura Ciccerone. And why the Jimmy who called you will keep trying to save himself from himself.

None of these fragments were meant to be autonomous

entities. They were meant to be pieces in a unified whole. When splitting occurs at the deepest possible level there is no longer any hope for fusion.

Okay. Consider yourself a lucky man, Salvo. No one ever gets the scoop straight from the Muse's mouth. Then again, you didn't either, did you?

Dead air followed, and I let it play until I was certain that Anna's voice was not coming back. My entire body reverberated with what the fuck and holy shit. To scream or to remain utterly silent amounted to the same thing. The only thing to do that seemed to make any sense was to rewind the tape and play it again.

As Anna sang the haunting lullaby, Byssan Lull, I remembered what she had said to me.

It doesn't mean anything. Byssan Lull is just Byssan Lull.

When the song ended, I clicked off the recorder. I was done listening.

I looked down at Keaton, who had planted himself in my lap, and restated—Byssan Lull is just Byssan Lull.

Yes, Keaton said, in a low sedate voice. You certainly took the long and scenic route in reaching that conclusion, didn't you?

Then he yawned, closed his eyes, and went to sleep.

Epilogue

It was a Tuesday evening.

I had just gotten back from dinner with Tania and Teddy. The T & T combo was three months in and still thriving.

As had become my habit, I fixed myself a cup Smoky Russian, then immediately set to work on Abyssinia. I had started working on it three weeks earlier, and had added fourteen new pages to Jimmy's original six.

I opened a couple of windows to let in the warm spring air.

Good for the soul, I announced to no one in particular.

Tea, pencils, notebook. I was ready to go. Then the phone rang.

Nine out of ten times—in that I was just about to start writing—I would have let the machine pick up. This was one of those rare tenths where my hand went to the phone, independent of my mind's habituations.

Hello, I said.

Still curious, Salvo.

I went cold inside.

Jimmy, my voice cracked.

Jimmy's dead, Salvo. I'm dead. Do you understand? I didn't understand. And I did. Didn't. And did.

These seemingly disparate elements canceled each other out, and I heard myself saying, in a small consoling voice— Yes, Jimmy, you're dead. Yes.

There was a click followed by a dialtone.

I sat quietly, staring at the phone. A part of me was curious to see who, if anyone, would pick up if I called Jimmy's old number. I ignored the urge and unplugged the phone.

Then I got down on my knees and did something I hadn't done since I was a young boy. I prayed. To whom or what it didn't matter.

I prayed that Jimmy would eventually be freed from whatever cycle was he was trapped in. I prayed that all the ghosts, living and dead, who wandered in the cold, would find a lasting sanctuary. I prayed for mercy in the most absolute and universal sense.

When I was done praying, I rose to my feet and went to my desk.

I understood clearly what I had to do.

I tore the fourteen pages I had written out of my notebook and threw them in the wastebasket.

Abyssinia belonged to Jimmy, not to me.

I paced around my apartment for a while. Thinking, not thinking. Eventually I made it back to my desk and sharpened a pencil. Then another. Okay, I said, and exhaled.

I opened my notebook and turned to a blank page. A new story, I thought. I wrote the line—There are many things that I am not—and realized it to be true.

About the Author

Originally from Brooklyn, NY, writer, poet, performer, and playwright, John Biscello, has lived in the high-desert grunge-wonderland of Taos, New Mexico since 2001.

He is the author of two novels, Broken Land, a Brooklyn Tale and Raking the Dust, and a collection of stories, Freeze Tag. Broken Land was named Underground Book Reviews 2014 Book of the Year. His third novel, Nocturne Variations, is due out November 2018 (Unsolicited Press).

Some of his primary influences and creative heroes include: Henry Miller, Charlie Chaplin, Ernest Hemingway, John Fante, Anais Nin, Jack Kerouac, Knut Hamsun, Yasunari Kawabata, William Saroyan, Dr. Seuss, Dylan Thomas, Julio Cortazar, Haruki Murakami, Paul Auster, Raymond Carver, Sylvia Plath, David Lynch, Billie Holiday, Miles Davis, and the list goes on and on and on.

About the Press

Unsolicited Press was founded in 2012. The team is a dedicated group of volunteer editors, designers, and producers seeking to publish exemplary fiction, poetry, and creative nonfiction. Learn more at www.unsolicitedpress.com.